Jane —

Ruby says your special and I hope you enjoy my books.

Don Ringfine

4/8/08

If We Never Meet Again This Side Of Heaven

...We'll Meet on that Beautiful Shore

❧❧

Don Swinford

Bloomington, IN   Milton Keynes, UK

authorHOUSE®

AuthorHouse™
1663 Liberty Drive, Suite 200
Bloomington, IN 47403
www.authorhouse.com
Phone: 1-800-839-8640

AuthorHouse™ UK Ltd.
500 Avebury Boulevard
Central Milton Keynes, MK9 2BE
www.authorhouse.co.uk
Phone: 08001974150

First published by AuthorHouse 9/8/2006

ISBN: 1-4259-5813-3 (sc)

Printed in the United States of America
Bloomington, Indiana

This book is printed on acid-free paper.

Dedication

This is dedicated to the people who have made a difference in my life. People who have contributed to my spiritual growth are at the top of the list, but there are also others who have influenced, nurtured, cared for, and loved me. Some are still living and others, I pray, have gone on to heaven. 1st.Corinthians 13: verse 13 says: "And now these three things remain: faith, hope, and love, but the greatest of these is love." So whether they helped me in my walk with God, or they have encouraged me in my pursuit of happiness, I thank them most of all for their love. There are many but two stand out: Ruby, my mother, and Marilyn, my wife. It is my prayer that all of us will once again be reunited in heaven some day.

A special thank you to my wife Marilyn, who designed the book cover.

Preface

This is a fictional story about a woman of modest beginnings who encountered many difficult trials in her life. Through faith she managed to rebound from adversity and develop an inner strength of character. She instilled her values in her children at an early age, and the story follows where this takes each of them. Her faith, hope, and love helped to sustain her and in the end were the driving force used to draw her family together.

A first cousin of mine who lost children during the depression inspired this story. She was the age of my parents, so I never knew her on a personal basis. I wasn't aware of the circumstances of her life until I was innocently drawn into her efforts to locate one of her children in 1964. What could her life have been like? That thought is what prompted me to create this fictional account of a mother in a dilemma.

Although it is fictional, it could have happened; and this is a depiction of the agony and trials a mother put in a situation where she couldn't raise her children might have had. The communities and school districts referred to here are real, as are many of the names used. Many are names from my childhood growing up in Coles County, Illinois. The use of the names is arbitrary, however; and, with only a few exceptions, do they have any basis in reality to the lives of friends and relatives living or dead.

Contents

Chapter 1

๏๛

Introduction

Things were different in rural America than they were in the cities at the beginning of the twentieth century. People were less sophisticated, but also more trusting. Children were free to roam around without their parents worrying about them. Everyone knew everyone, and any stranger in town stood out. Frances liked that about this small town of Ashmore, Illinois. Her parents had moved around quite a bit, and it was hard to get accepted by kids when you were always the new kid in town. She liked this school because there were more children and she felt less noticeable than she had in other places. She was always self-conscious about her looks, and that had resulted in her being extremely shy. After being here for two years, she was pretty sure she'd finish her education right here, an eighth grade education. No one ever talked about her getting more schooling.

She was a preacher's kid, and it wasn't too unusual to have moved around a lot. The church was growing here, so it looked like they might just be here for a while. Ever since the Reverend Billy Sunday had held a revival over in Charleston the summer before, the number of churchgoers had increased steadily. She'd seen several new faces in their church, and the members seemed to like her daddy. She knew her momma was hoping the moving was over.

Their home wasn't much, but Momma kept it clean. The church rented it from Mr. Kearn for them instead of paying her daddy extra to find his own house. She always heard that preacher's didn't get much pay so that is why they gave them a house to live in. The house had last been used to store corn and farm equipment, but they had put a new roof on and added a porch. The people from the church were good about giving her momma old clothing to be fixed up for the children. She couldn't remember the last new dress she had, but her momma did a good job of altering clothes for all of them and kept everything clean. Daddy often said, "Cleanliness is next to Godliness."

The family consisted of her parents, the Reverend William McGrew and his wife Mary, and Frances' siblings Robert, Willis, and Evangeline. Robert was the older brother, and Willis and Evangeline were both younger than Frances.

Frances didn't have friends. Besides being shy, she didn't think much of herself. There was only one girl at school that she felt comfortable talking to and that was Sally Trapp. Sally was a year younger, and she seemed to have the same problem mixing with other kids as Frances did. She lived about a mile outside of town with her dad and two brothers. The flu epidemic that had already killed so many had taken her mother the past winter. She was really needed at home to take care of things and felt lucky that she even got to come to school. Sally was prettier than she, Frances thought, but her clothes were not always clean. She only wore shoes when it was really cold, and then they didn't fit her feet very well. They had only started talking to each other because they were normally the two left out of everything, but Frances was beginning to like her.

Frances' younger brother and sister were two and four years behind her in school, and she thought them brighter and prettier than she was. They definitely were more popular with the kids, and the teachers seemed to give them a lot more attention than they ever gave her. Her daddy had always favored them, too, and showed them a lot more attention than he ever did her. When he was in a good mood, he'd sometimes bounce them on his knee, sing, and play games with them. When he spoke to Frances, it was normally to tell her to do something. He often pointed out to her that she was old enough to be more help to her mother than she was. A time or two he'd added, "If you don't pay attention and try harder, you'll have a hard time in this world." Once Frances overheard him tell some of his friends that she was the runt of the family. She still felt the hurt, but at least she didn't get the beatings that Robert and Willis would get from time to time. He didn't believe in sparing the rod and spoiling the child obviously. Most of the time, Frances felt he just ignored her.

Robert was the older brother and a hero to Willis and Evangeline. He already had an eighth grade education and while he didn't have regular work, he managed to find enough work to keep him busy most of the time. He could do no wrong, but let it be known early in life to everyone who was listening that he wasn't going to be a preacher. He and his daddy got along well enough, but he definitely was the independent soul. Some jobs he took would keep him away from home for a week at a time, but on Sunday he'd normally be in church with the rest of them. Frances' mom missed him when he was gone because he helped her with heavier chores. Those that her husband never quite had time for. She had to learn that his days at home were numbered now, and she would have to learn to cope without him. He was a grown young man of seventeen.

At times it seemed that the Reverend had more time for his flock than he did for his own family. That's what their church called the members. He was the shepherd, and they were the flock. For the church members he was on call day or night. Being a preacher's wife was tough, and Frances' mother (who was only thirty-four) appeared much older of late. At the birth of Evangeline something had gone wrong which made it impossible for her to have more children, but as the years went on she also seemed to tire more easily. Sometimes she had to stop in the middle of the day to rest more than once. The last couple of years she always wore a big bonnet when she worked the garden, and her face always had a flush about it. Frances noticed how much her daddy prayed for her at times. The people called them the Reverend and Mrs. McGrew. Frances was proud of them and loved them, but she didn't feel she counted for much with her daddy.

Mrs. McGrew was the oldest of nine children, and several of them still lived in Coles County. That's where Ashmore and the county seat of Charleston were located. She didn't see them very often, but her momma's youngest brother, Adren, lived just five miles down by the river bottoms with his family and came by to visit more than most. He was Frances' uncle, but she was in fact two years older. He was born when his daddy was fifty-five, and he and the McGrew kids had grown up together. Adren was the same age as Willis, and they were friends. He was Frances' favorite because he was cute and friendly. He always treated her well and took time to talk to her.

Frances and Sally Trapp were getting better acquainted all the time. One day Frances told her, "I'm short like my momma, but she's pretty and I'm not. Daddy said she was the prettiest girl in the county when he met her. I guess my looks are a throwback to my Grandma McGrew. I never knew her, but I've seen a tintype picture of her. I guess I do resemble her. Our faces are too round and fat. We're pug-nosed and our mouths just don't seem to go with the rest of our face. We both have big gaps between our front teeth. Daddy never talks about her. He said his dad died young, maybe in the war. I'm not sure because he doesn't seem to want to talk much about any of his family. He has some, but we never see them. I know enough not to press him for more when he doesn't volunteer it."

Chapter 2

❦❧

Growing Up

In three months Frances' formal schooling would be over. She had no idea what she would be doing with the rest of her life. She felt her possibilities were very limited. Marriage was all but out of the question. Most young women in rural America married young and had families, but she had never even had a boy show the least bit of interest in her. There was no one she could talk to except her momma, and she had enough to deal with. They had never talked about things like that. She wasn't very well prepared for life after school, and in a way she wished it would never end.

Sally Trapp had missed several days of school and Frances was missing her. She came back one day, riding up behind her dark-haired brother on the back of an old plow horse. Frances had seen Orville before. He rode right up to her and let Sally off. He told Frances that Sally had sprained her ankle bad and hadn't been able to get to school, but that he'd be back for her in the evening but might be late. Frances helped Sally to her desk. Sally said Orville had been nice to her and had borrowed the horse to bring her. She told Frances she had missed seeing her. From then on they began to talk and share more together. Frances began to confide in Sally about her fear of the future. Sally said her problem was that her daddy wasn't well, and her older brothers Orville and Raymond had taken things over. She loved her big brothers,

5

but she didn't have anyone to really share girl or women things with. Her brothers were big and strong, but neither had stayed in school more than four years. They could write their names, but other than that they didn't have much to show for their education. Frances and Sally grew to depend on each other, but neither had much experience to draw on. This only added to their feelings of inadequacy.

As spring approached, Frances got to see Orville more often as he'd show up at school two or three times a week to bring Sally or pick her up. Once in awhile he'd sit and talk with just the two of them, and when the early flowers started blooming he brought Frances a bunch to say thanks for befriending his little sister. Frances blushed, but was secretly flattered when Willis and Evangeline began to tease her about Orville. She was having her own fantasies about him and looked forward to the days he'd show up.

Her teacher, Mrs. Eads, taught the upper three classes. Frances thought she was very sweet; but she was so busy with those who spoke up and asked a lot of questions that she rarely called on Frances. Frances just tried to do what she said to do and not be a problem. Once or twice she'd have Frances help Sally with her math problems, so Frances guessed she was satisfied with her work. Teaching looked like it would be a satisfying job, but Frances couldn't imagine trying to get some of the older kids to mind. Some were much bigger than she was, and she couldn't be that brave.

There was less than a month left in school when one of the porch boards broke under Sally at school. She hurt her ankle that was still weak from the sprain. Mrs. Eads was wondering what to do when Frances volunteered to help her walk home. It was only a mile away, and there would be plenty of time before dark. She agreed and let the two of them out early to get started. Sally leaned on Frances a little to take some of the weight off, and they started down the road. Frances had never actually seen Sally's home because it was back up a wooded path. When she saw it, she was shocked at how small and dilapidated it was. It made her feel better in a way about what the preacher's family was living in, although she felt badly for Sally.

As they approached the house, they could see Orville with the horse and plow in the clearing nearest the yard coming their way. No one else was around; so they waited until he got there. Then Sally explained what happened. He told Frances to wait while he helped Sally inside, then he'd give her a ride home. Frances said that wasn't necessary, but he was back in a minute. He pulled the plow harness off the old horse and insisted she climb up behind him.

They started back toward town; but instead of following the road, Orville guided the horse up the riverbed that ran in the direction of the town. It was a slow easy gait with Frances hanging onto his waist so as not to slide off the bare broad-backed sweaty animal that was more accustomed to the plow than it was to riders. They had not gone very far when at a bend to the river, they saw a clump of the prettiest spring flowers. Orville wanted to get down and collect them so Frances had to get off, too. He picked the flowers and handed them to her, and then sat down on a log near the water's edge.

He wanted to talk and began by telling how he missed his mom. He used to bring her the early spring flowers to brighten the dark, damp shell of a house they lived in. His remembrances of her made Frances sad for him. When he encouraged her to sit by him on the log, she sat quietly listening to him tell about his boyhood. Like her, she sensed that he had missed a lot.

In the shade of the trees, the breeze seemed much cooler. He noticed that she shivered a time or two before he put his arm around her shoulders to warm her. She sat rigid, as this had never happened to her before. She didn't know how to act, but she liked it. A man not her brother, actually touching her and talking tenderly to her. She'd had fantasies, but this was the real thing. She didn't know what to do, so she just sat still and listened.

In a few minutes his talk was more about him, about his needing and wanting a home and family of his own. His daddy had been his age when he got married, and Orville knew he could handle the responsibilities that came with a wife and family.   He stroked her hair as he told her she was the first girl he could ever talk to this way because he'd gotten to know her. She had been so sweet to Sally, and he just knew that Frances was mature and had a beautiful heart and would make a wonderful wife and mother. She was astonished when he reached down and brushed her lips with his. After she got over the initial shock, she instinctively responded the second time he did so. Soon she found herself locked in his strong arms in a warm embrace.

Nothing or no one had prepared her for this. Before long they were lying on the grassy bank, and he was moving his hands up and down her body. All at once she was aware that this wasn't right. She had heard enough of her daddy's sermons to know good girls didn't do this. She tried pulling back and telling Orville that this was wrong. He fondled her and kept insisting that it was right because he loved her so much. He said everything was okay and that they would be very happy and she would be his best girl forever. She resisted but was confused and amazed that someone cared for her this much. Only when she felt a sharp pain did she realize that they had gone too far. She had become one of those women that the Bible called harlots.

She was in the state of mild shock when Orville pulled her to her feet. He helped her back on the horse, all the while pledging his love. At the same time he was asking her not to tell any one about this as she was so young and people wouldn't understand their love and would only make problems for them.

The trip back to town was a blur. When Frances got home, no one was around. She lay down and tried to nap. Her mind was racing. It was a strange and confusing day. She wondered how soon it would be before she went to hell. After a while her mom called for help in fixing dinner, and she got up and went quietly to her chores. The other kids were home and Dad was late. Everything seemed very normal. She'd survived so far, and out there was someone who loved her. Surely that meant something. This day had changed everything for her. She knew she'd been bad, but it didn't seem all that wrong.

Things were normal at school the next morning, except Sally was missing, apparently at home nursing her injured ankle. When she came back the next day, she walked in by herself. When Frances asked about Orville, she said Mr. Campbell had needed him on the other farm down the road. It was about ten miles away, and he'd probably be gone until they got the plowing and planting finished. Frances tried to concentrate on her schoolwork, but it wasn't easy. She didn't want to draw any special attention to herself, especially now. She felt like she was wearing a scarlet letter on her chest like Hester in the book "Scarlet Letter." She wished she'd never read that book.

Frances had invited Sally to go to church services before, but Sally had not been able to come. The Sunday before the last week of school, she said she could come. Frances was so happy and planned to meet her at the end of the street and walk with her. They sat on the back pew. It meant so much to have her one true friend with her at a time when she had so much on her mind. They held hands the whole time. Although Sally didn't know many of the songs, she sang the songs she did know with a clear and beautiful voice. She said she missed going to church with her momma and that she was going to do better in the future, even if her dad and brothers thought it was a waste of time. She liked Frances' church.

They were standing outside talking after the services when Mrs. Percey came over. She was old and Frances didn't remember Mr. Percey, so thought he'd probably been dead a long time. They had no children as far as Frances knew, and Mrs. Percey had always gone out of her way to be sweet to her. In her hand was a paper sack, which she handed to Frances and said, "For your graduation." She asked Sally if she was graduating, and Sally had shyly told her that she had another year. "Open it," Mrs. Percey said. Frances took out a yellow and blue apron that Mrs. Percey had made for her. Tears collected in Frances' eyes as she held it up. It had been a long time since she'd had anything this pretty, and new besides. She hugged Mrs. Percey tightly.

On the last day of school Frances was given a letter of completion from the eighth grade. She clutched it tightly in her hand as she carried it directly home to her momma. She had completed one phase of her life. Still there was no Orville, and she wasn't sure what the next stage held for her. He did send a message with Sally that he was proud of her and that he'd call on her when the workload let up. He said he missed her. Sally said he talked about her all the time when he was at home, and she kidded Frances about him.

Chapter 3

಄ ಄

Facts of Life

Frances' mom had knitted her a sweater for graduation, and her dad had bought a new Bible and given her his old one. Other than that, life went on as usual. Summer wasn't the time for rest but rather for real work, as Frances soon found out. The younger kids had their chores, but Frances was busy looking for and finding work to make money.

Some of the wealthier church members would pay her to clean house and do laundry for them. She'd promptly turn the small change they gave her over to her momma. About once a week she'd notice a special treat for dinner that they didn't normally have. She had her first banana about then and always remembered the taste of that first one. It amazed her that it had come from such a far distance and could still be so good. Her momma did say that she was putting a little of her money aside for Frances to use when and where she wanted.

One day was much like another until a day in late June. Frances was scrubbing floors at Mrs. Temple's house. She could hear the conversation coming from the parlor where Mrs. Temple and two lady friends were. They were discussing the problems that the Caldwell family over in Charleston was having. It seemed that the banker's daughter had gotten pregnant out of wedlock, and the rascal who did it wouldn't marry her. Mrs. Temple remarked that she just couldn't understand how decent, upright people could let their pretty young daughters grow up so ignorant of the consequences of immoral sex. They were talking in more detail than Frances had ever heard. She couldn't help but think that it might be a good idea for them to explain the facts of life to their homely daughters as well.

As she was walking back home that evening after a long tiring day and twenty-five cents for her efforts, she still had that conversation on her mind. She was walking slowly and had just rounded some trees and had her house in view when there, striding directly toward her was Orville. She hadn't seen him in nearly two months since that afternoon, and she had to catch her breath. He seemed to be angry, and only when he saw her did he slow down his pace and let the frown leave his face. She was so surprised that she was speechless, but slowly smiled because she truly was happy to see him again. The Devil hadn't claimed her yet, and the look in his eyes let her know that he was happy to see her, too. He took her hand and started telling her he hadn't been around because of the places he had been sent to work. Frances heard her father yelling at her to get home immediately, and she was confused about what to do. All she was doing was talking, and here her father was yelling at the top of his lungs. Most of the town probably heard him. Orville finally said, "I guess I'd best go on for now. Your dad and me had words."

She was still wondering what was going on as she hurried on home watching Orville's retreating back. She was nearing the door when her dad told her to get into the house and sit down at the table. She did as she was told. He didn't pull up a chair but began to pace back and forth. He was saying that he wouldn't have his family associating with the likes of the Trapp boys who were heathens. They hadn't darkened the door of a church for five years, long before their mother passed. They blamed God for her death and, furthermore, they weren't ever going to start coming to church. That heathen had said that right after he had asked to court his eldest daughter. Her dad had told him to get out and stay away. He said to Frances in anger, "You may not be much, but you're a sight better than those Trapps. If I ever see him near you, I'll take the leather to him. That's a two way street, sister. If you ever tail around after the likes of him, you'll be searching for a new roof over your head. He has blasphemed the Holy Ghost and will end up in the lake of fire for eternity." She sat speechless and motionless and didn't dare to question him about the love and forgiveness that she'd recently been reading about in his old Bible. She was at a loss. What could she do now? The next few days she steered clear of him because he was doing a lot of scowling when she was around.

Around her birthday, when she was turning fourteen, she could sense something was different. The cycle that had just started a couple of years before (her momma had explained it as normal) didn't appear normal anymore. In fact, a couple of months had passed and, with the education she had gotten from Mrs. Temple's parlor talk, she was beginning to understand the facts of life. She guessed that being homely didn't change some facts. She began to lose sleep and wonder what she was going to do. As the preacher's daughter, she didn't dare talk to any of the older girls because they were sure to tell someone and only the Lord knew what would happen to her daddy and his job, not to think of her momma's shame. Only after some time did she figure out an excuse to go to Charleston where she'd heard you could borrow reading material at a library. She had a subject that she really needed to check out.

One day in late July she caught a free ride with Mr. Murtaugh's grocery wagon to Charleston with the dollar and a half of her earnings that her momma had saved for her. She went on the pretense of shopping. When she got there, a person she asked pointed her to the library. There the veil of ignorance was lowered.

When she got back to Ashmore, she didn't even stop at her house. She kept right on going down the road a mile to the shady lane leading back to Orville and Sally's house. As she approached, Sally saw her and ran to greet her; glad to take a break from the wood chopping she was attempting to do. She was the only one home, so they spent a couple of hours telling of their summer until Sally had to start fixing dinner for her dad and brothers. Although evening was approaching, Frances wasn't about to budge before Orville got home and she had a chance to tell him what had happened.

She helped Sally with the meal, and before long noises outside told them that the men were arriving. Mr. Trapp came in the door first and stopped short when he saw the visitor. He was a frail, unkempt man with tobacco stains on his mouth and clothes. Before he said anything, Orville and Raymond came in. Orville immediately came over to her and gave her a hug. He told his dad and brother that this was the

13

girl he had talked about, Sally's friend. Raymond, who wasn't much older than Frances, managed a smile and said hello, but Mr. Trapp just continued to stare. She then told Orville she needed to talk to him, and he led her outside and away from the house. He began telling her how much he had missed her and how he had been dying to come to town, but hadn't wanted to have trouble with her family. It was then she said, "We have trouble." He stopped and looked at her. With tears in her eyes, she told him she was going to have a baby. Stunned silence followed. She continued weeping for what seemed an eternity until he asked, "Are you sure?" She could only say that her body was changing but she hadn't been checked out. She didn't know what to do or whom she could trust. Orville took her hand in his and looking her in the eyes said, "Now your dad will have to accept me. I need to talk to Raymond first, but we need to go to town and see your daddy together. I want to do the right thing."

They went back into the house, and Orville took Raymond aside for some serious talk. In a few minutes they went over to some bedrolls in the corner and searched through them. He came over, took Frances' hand, and told his dad and Sally that he had to go to town and that Raymond would explain. Sally handed a piece of bread and slice of meat to Orville as he guided Frances out the door. He offered Frances some of his dinner on the way to town, but she wasn't hungry. It was still light but they had to hurry, as she was sure her mom was missing her by now.

Not much was said except Orville repeated several times his intentions of marrying her and how happy they would be. He wished it hadn't happened this way, but at least now they could get on with their lives. He said Raymond had helped him out with a loan and that they could get married right away, tonight if possible.

When they got to Ashmore, the wicks in the lamps were already lit and her mom was feeding the kids at the table. Her dad wasn't home yet as she led Orville into the house. Her mom just stopped and stared at them with her hands in her apron. Frances thought it best if Mom would come outside with them where the kids wouldn't be listening. She followed along slowly, still unsure of whether she wanted to be with them or not. Frances asked her where daddy was and she could only shrug her shoulders. It was Tuesday and he didn't have any special schedule or services, so he could be anywhere. Frances hesitated. She didn't know what to say. She fidgeted and struggled for words until she finally blurted out, "Orville and I want to get married." Her momma's hands flew to her mouth and her lips were quivering. Frances repeated herself again and her momma said, "Your dad won't allow this." She collected herself and went on to say that Orville should leave before the Reverend showed up and she didn't want him upset. She turned to leave, and Frances cried out to her, "Momma, I'm going to have a baby." Her momma froze in her tracks and, even though the light had gotten bad, Frances thought she saw the color drain from her face. Her momma's next words were, "You can't be. You don't know anything about having babies. You're not much more than a baby yourself." With grief in her eyes she studied her little girl's body. Then Frances saw the dawning in her eyes as she whispered, "Oh, my God."

It was then that Orville said, "I love her. I'll take care of her and she'll be happy." Just as momma was saying, "What will your daddy do?" a surrey rounded the trees and a man brought the horse to a halt near them. The passenger, Reverend McGrew got out of the surrey and looked at them in total disbelief. He said, "Thanks Tom for the ride and I hope the misses gets to feeling better. I'll be praying for her." Tom then drove on, leaving the Reverend standing like a statue only twenty feet away with not a hint of coming closer. Orville said, "Reverend McGrew, I've been thinking about what you said to me and I am giving it all some serious thought." Her daddy said slowly, "Well, that's a start. Why don't you go on now and maybe come by the church tomorrow night where we can talk and pray about this some more." Orville hesitated again and said, "I've thought about it. I love your daughter and want to marry her right away." All at once the fire came back into the Reverend's eyes, and he said that his daughter wasn't marrying anybody and least of all a heathen. He now walked toward the couple threateningly, even though he was a head shorter than Orville. He reached out to pull Frances away from Orville's side when her momma in a whisper said, "She's pregnant." His hand stopped in mid-air as he gasped for air. His next move was to lunge at Orville, but Orville quickly moved and he went to the ground in a heap. As Orville reached to help him up, he took a wild swing that missed. His face was all wadded up in a terrible grimace. Frances blurted out to him, "Daddy, I love him." He turned his head her way with a look that made her feel ill in her stomach. His next words to her were, "You're no good and I want you out of my house now and forever." With that he got up and stumbled into the house, leaving her momma standing there weeping and Frances and Orville stunned. Finally her momma said, "Wait here, I'll go try."

They stood there for about ten minutes and couldn't hear what was going on. Frances went to her knees. The kids came out and ran to their sister with startled looks and both gave her hugs. A yell from the house told them to get back inside right now. They passed their momma in the doorway with a bundle in her arms. She was crying as she handed Frances the small bundle that held most of her clothing in it and pressed a little change into her palm. Frances noted that her Bible was missing. Her mom said for them to go quickly before Robert showed up and caused more problems. She said she'd find Frances if she could change her daddy's mind, but she was afraid he wouldn't. When Frances asked for her Bible, she said her daddy had grabbed it from her as she was leaving the house. She touched Frances' cheek and went inside. Orville helped Frances to her feet from where she had been kneeling and led her off.

They were walking past the church when she finally thought to ask, "Where are we going?" Orville seemed at a loss and was struggling for an answer when she suggested they sit down on the step of the church for a while and pray about it. They sat quietly for a while before she took his hand and asked him to pray with her. In her silent prayer, she asked for guidance and mercy. As they sat there, she felt a strength that she had not experienced before. She sank to her knees. With a conviction she could never remember ever having before, she prayed for her parents. She finished with the thought, "If we never meet again this side of heaven, we'll meet on that beautiful shore."

With strength she didn't know she had, she jumped up and pulled Orville to his feet. She explained that she had been in Charleston that day and had seen the courthouse. That's where she knew they must go to get married. He only protested a little by saying, "That's five miles away," but he agreed to go. To go to his father's house was just adding miles to the journey he knew they must make, so they started down the road to Charleston. Orville said he hoped they could get married on the eight dollars he had. Frances didn't mention the dollar plus change that she had.

Charleston was pretty much asleep as they approached it about ten o'clock in the evening. They walked along, hand in hand, and most of the time they had their own private thoughts and fears to think about. Orville had worked hard all day and was really tired. Because it was a beautiful July evening and because of the stress of the day, they decided to bed down in a partially grown cornfield using some young stalks for a bed and Frances' bundle for a pillow. Frances had found an inner peace in prayer that surprised her, and she slept soundly that night. Orville was more troubled but didn't bother her as she slept.

They woke at sunrise and managed to enter town without any one noticing where they had come from. A small restaurant serving breakfast was open, and the large hot breakfast was the most delicious she had ever tasted. She had missed supper the night before, but now she had a huge appetite and she wondered if that was a part of it. They took their time eating, knowing nothing else would be open for a while, and talked about everything. It was time to get to know each other. Well, perhaps past time, but they had a lot of catching up to do. They talked about what they would do and where they would do it. Other than the fact that they needed a license, neither had any idea of what else was necessary. She mentioned to Orville that she didn't even know how old he was. As it turned out, he had just turned eighteen. He did tell her that maybe she'd better not give her true age to the courthouse people. It seemed he had heard that people had to be eighteen to be married.

They walked the streets and talked about what they would do until they noticed people beginning to come and go from the courthouse. They went in the front door and asked the first person they saw who to see to get married. They were pointed to a desk in a corner where a small man with glasses sat. He asked them several questions and when he asked her age, she lied and said eighteen. Her momma's words were still in her ears, "You're still just a baby." At the same time she made a silent repentance for her lie.

The papers were filled out. The man asked Orville for two dollars, which he paid. Frances asked the man if they were married now, and he chuckled and said, "No, you'll have to see the judge or a preacher for that."

They walked around again for a while to think that over. They decided they just couldn't take the chance a preacher might know her daddy and try to contact him. Instead they walked back to the courthouse and asked to see the judge. It was a couple of hours before they saw him, and he pronounced them man and wife, for better or for worse. They walked out the front door into the world, man and wife, with nowhere to go.

Over breakfast, Orville had told her about a Mr. Snider whom he had met while working over near Oakland in a place called Canaan. It wasn't a town, just a school district name. Mr. Snider apparently liked Orville and told him that he might have some part-time work if he was ever available. They didn't have many choices, and living in or near Ashmore just wasn't possible anymore. They began asking around for anyone going toward Oakland. It was only about sixteen miles, but that was a lot when you're on foot. Orville stayed near the gas station asking most everybody, but it was well into the afternoon before he found a ride. In return he bought the man two gallons of gas.

When they went through Ashmore on their way to Oakland, Frances kept her head down so that she couldn't see or be seen. This was a new life, and she had to put ugly times behind her. Before they got to Oakland, Orville had the man stop at a road headed west and thanked him for the ride. They were afoot again but Orville seemed to know where he was headed. They had walked about a mile and a half when Orville pointed to a nice white house sitting on a rise. "That," he said, "is Mr. Snider's."

They were lucky to find Mr. Snider at home. He seemed glad to see Orville but somewhat surprised he had a wife. Orville showed him the marriage papers and was congratulated by Mr. Snider. Mrs. Snider offered them some milk and cookies. Frances hadn't eaten since breakfast and enjoyed the snacks. The women talked inside while Mr. Snider and Orville went out on the porch to talk business. Frances found out the Snider children were mostly grown with only a sixteen year old still at home, but today he was at some activity at the high school in Oakland. Mrs. Snider asked Frances questions without being too nosey, and Frances told about her dad disowning her because she wanted to marry Orville. She didn't mention anything about a baby though. Mrs. Snider said she hoped they could patch it up because a girl only has one set of parents. Frances agreed.

When Mr. Snider and Orville came back inside, Orville told Frances that Mr. Snider had been nice enough to ask them to stay the night. Mrs. Snider said they had spare bedrooms and that they were welcome. Mr. Snider said he expected there were things that Orville and Frances wanted to discuss, so he and his wife went to the kitchen, leaving them alone.

Orville explained, "We've gotten lucky. He gave me a job starting tomorrow and has an idea for a place to live that he'll show us after supper." The Sniders were being so wonderful. Frances knew that she would love them forever for what they did to make their wedding evening so special. Life was certainly brighter now than they had been that morning.

Later, with Mr. Snider driving the rig, they took a ride over the hill about a mile to a place that by moonlight more resembled a lean-to than a house. Mr. Snider explained that he would furnish the logs so they could make it a real home before winter set in. She and Orville were just thankful they had a roof over their head. When they got back to the house, Mrs. Snider led Frances to her bedroom in the back of the house. When she noticed the meager contents of Frances' bundle, she insisted that Frances take the silky nightgown that she offered. She told Frances that she and her husband were going to sleep upstairs. Frances resisted taking their room, but Mrs. Snider insisted and wouldn't hear of anything else. Orville and Frances spent their honeymoon night in the most beautiful bedroom she had ever seen. Wearing the nightgown, for the first time in her life she didn't feel ugly.

Chapter 4

❧ ❧

Starting Family Life

Their first home, a one-room house, only had a bedroll borrowed from the Sniders and one straight chair that first day, but they were home. They collected a few pots and pans and a small cook stove, along with utensils, within a week. The second week Orville was hauling logs home to start an addition. They didn't have very much money, but the Sniders saw to it that they had enough food and that Orville was paid each Saturday. Frances' appetite and cravings were definitely growing, and sometimes it was hard to keep food in the house. By the early frost, their eight-by-ten home had grown another eight feet, complete with roof and a partition to separate the bedroom from the kitchen.

Raymond came over on weekends to help out and brought them the news from home. Sally came with him one time after school had started, and brought Frances a quilt she had made for their wedding present. She was happy for them, but Frances could tell that these recent months without Orville had been tough for her.

Orville was busy seven days a week during the harvest season, but things slowed down around Thanksgiving. About that time they had their first trip to Oakland in a rig borrowed from the Sniders. Frances liked the town a lot and noticed that people were even beginning to treat her as a grown up. Shopping for things for her home was a new experience for her. She didn't have much, but she did a good job getting the most for her money.

After about a month after they were married, she started hinting to Orville that she's like to find a church to go to. There was one only a mile away. He said getting the place ready for cold weather was more important and that's how he wanted to spend Sundays. She'd find a quiet spot and pray each day but missed going to church and reading the Bible. The baby was growing inside her and these things were becoming even more important to her. She decided that she needed to find a way to go to church whether Orville went or not.

Most days were pretty lonely for her because there were only about five houses within a mile, and like them, everyone was just trying to survive. They didn't have a garden to tend but Frances spent a lot of time trying to make their place look better. Orville got some whitewash for the outside, and Mrs. Snider had shared some old remnants of cloth and worn out shirts with her to use inside. She did the best she could, making a curtain for the door and things that she would need for the baby. Before she got too big, she picked tomatoes for a week on a neighboring farm. The few dollars she made helped get things they needed very badly, and that was about everything.

She confided in Mrs. Snider that she was pregnant, but suspected her new friend had known for some time. It wasn't long before the wagon came over the hill with an old crib, diapers, and some baby clothes that Mrs. Snider said she would have no use for again. She sat with Frances one whole afternoon and told her about motherhood and what she could expect in childbirth. As it turned out, there was a midwife living less than two miles away, and she offered to talk to her for Frances the next time she saw her. In talking it over, the best they could figure, the baby would come about the last week of January. She taught Frances so much and, after the crops were in, she stopped by at least once a week to check on her. Frances had never had this kind of attention and began to feel more secure. Orville was wonderful to her. Even he said she had a certain glow about her and it looked like having babies agreed with her.

There was some early weather around Thanksgiving and they learned real fast where all the cracks were in their house. They caulked the best they could with clay and old rags, but it still was a challenge to keep warm with the cook stove. Frances had done what she could in cutting wood, but it was pretty obvious they would need a lot more wood than what they had been able to cut to make it to spring. She wasn't much help to Orville in that regard after September.

There was a break in the weather just before Christmas. Frances was carrying wash water to the house from the pump while Orville chopped wood when they had a surprise visitor. Uncle Adren came riding in on horseback, and she was so happy to see him that she hugged him hard. When he had visited his sister, her momma, over the years he had seemed more like a brother than an uncle. This tall dark haired handsome twelve-year-old boy had to be one of the friendliest boys Frances had ever known. He and Orville hit it off well and, despite his kidding Frances about her big belly, she was excited to see him and hear news of her momma and family. He said they were doing okay and that Willis had encouraged him to look her up when he could.

He only lived about four miles away in Yellowhammer, another school district, but those were tough miles in the wintertime. The roads could get pretty bad. His daddy had his own farm, about 80 acres, and Adren was kept pretty busy and had stopped school after six years to help. He stayed all day Saturday and Frances got to fix a guest supper for the first time. He promised to come back when the baby was born. As he rode away, Frances just felt that this was one family she could always count on.

Her Christmas was made really special when Orville surprised her by going to Sunday services with her. He borrowed a rig from Mr. Snider, and they went to church in style. The people treated them real nice and she got to meet Mrs. Kite, the midwife that Mrs. Snider had told her about. She told Frances how and when to contact her. Frances went home happy, thinking that after the baby came, this going to church and meeting new people was going to be a normal thing. There wasn't any tree in their home for Christmas, but her joy was complete when Orville handed her a bundle with a Bible in it. Not a new Bible but an extra one that the Sniders had found for her. There would never be another Christmas like that one. Her husband proved to her how much he cared for her by giving her something that she would always cherish. She had made him a pie.

The good Lord was watching over them the second week in January when a terrible ice storm hit. Tree limbs everywhere were breaking off with the weight of the ice. Orville had gone to the Sniders that morning, just before it started, to do the milking. Before noon there was a glaze of ice everywhere, and she began to feel the pain of contractions. In less than two hours they had become so regular and often that Frances was sure she was about to have her baby all alone without any help. She was heating water on the stove when Orville came into the house, and she all but collapsed in his arms. Because of the weather, Mr. Snider had insisted he take the wagon and team, and that saved the day for her. He bundled her up and put her in the back of the wagon. Sliding side to side on the road they headed to the home of the midwife, just in time for their son to be born.

He had lots of black hair, and Frances insisted that he was Orville Jr. They stayed at Mrs. Kite's overnight due to the weather, and the next day the sun broke through as the Trapp family returned home. Orville Jr. may have come a week or two early, but he was a beautiful healthy boy. Mr. Snider understood why Orville had missed the milking the next morning, and his wife sent him over with a dinner for their homecoming. She also sent a bundle containing two beautiful new baby blankets. The date was January 10, 1916.

Ten days later the new mother was nursing her baby when she heard what sounded like a car motor outside. The weather was well above freezing by then. When she answered the door, she couldn't believe her eyes. It was her momma, Robert, Willis, and Evangeline. Unknown to her, Orville had sent word and they were there for her, and to meet their newest relative. This was the first she had seen them in over six months. Tears streamed down her face as she hugged and shared her precious bundle with them. They brought baby gifts and food, and for a couple of hours the cares of the world were left behind. It would have only been more perfect had her daddy and Orville been there. Her mom explained that it couldn't happen too often, but when she could she'd come back. Frances understood her loyalties and was thankful that at least her momma had forgiven her. Willis was the first to call Orville Jr. "Orvie," and the rest picked up on it. From that day on he was Orvie.

Chapter 5

❧❧

The Early Years

The days and months flew by for the new parents and their growing son. They were happy, and the new experiences of watching their baby develop brought a new joy everyday. There was no shortage of work and, although there was never enough cash, they managed to accumulate and even expand their holdings as Mr. Snider gave them the materials to build a small shed out back for a cow and some small equipment. He even let them have a small plot on the edge of the field behind the house for a garden. They were enjoying the good life. There was a sincere and warm affection between the Sniders and Trapps, and it was as though the Trapps were taking the place of some of their family that had married and moved on.

It was in July of 1917 that their world changed again. While working in the hot sun cutting the corn and weeds out of the beans, Mr. Snider had a stroke and died in the field while Orville was with him. It was a terrible loss. Orville's father had passed the previous winter, and this double loss depressed him for quite awhile. It also put an extra strain on him to do all the work that needed to be done.

Finally, about harvest time, Mrs. Snider's oldest son John and his family moved in with her to take over the farm. While he was a nice man, things began to change. After the crops were in, John told Orville that he wouldn't be able to use him as much as his dad had because he'd be doing more himself in the future out of necessity. The Trapps could stay in the house, but there wouldn't be much work for Orville until plowing time in the spring. Mrs. Snider had taught Frances how to can vegetables, so they did have food stored for the winter. Orville could only pick up odd and end jobs from other farmers in December and January and most of the time had a lot of idle time.

Frances' momma had visited three or four times since the baby was born. The news was that Willis had gone on to high school because he wanted to become a teacher. Momma was very proud of him. Robert had decided to venture out and had gone to Colorado to find work and live. Evangeline was at home and doing well. She wouldn't share with Frances anything about her daddy or the church. She thought her dad made her mother pledge not to do so before he'd agree for her to visit. Momma and Orville never had much to say to each other, but she was crazy for Orvie. She'd hold him about all the time during her visits. A couple of times Uncle Adren had driven the wagon for her. Momma called him Buck because he had grown to be such a strapping boy, nearly six foot tall. They both did little things to make the Trapp place homey. On one occasion Buck and Orville went fishing down on the Embarrass River together. They liked to mushroom hunt together also.

The people in Canaan didn't know much about the outside world except to know there was fighting in Europe. Some of Frances' uncles had already gone to war and other neighbors and friends from church were talking about it. In February 1918, Orville started talking about joining to make some money because there wasn't any work. Frances didn't know anything about war and never saw a newspaper but she didn't want him to leave. In the end, though, he said it was best for them. With an agreement from the Sniders that allowed his wife to stay in the house, Orville joined the Army. He said a year in the Army would help financially.

By April he was gone, along with Mrs. Snider's youngest son. Orville asked Adren to look in on his family as often as possible. He knew that Orvie was a healthy happy toddler that would fill his wife's days and minimize her loneliness.

Orville had the garden plowed before he left, so when it warmed Frances was able to get the garden in. Days were filled with routine, and she was so busy with Orvie that the weeks slipped by quickly. She got a letter about once a week from Orville who was over in Missouri training. He said in ways it was a lot easier than some of the farming he had done. He especially enjoyed learning to shoot the big rifle they had and was among the best in his group of men at it. They called him a sharp shooter. He didn't know anything for sure, but suspected after training that he'd probably get to come home for a short visit. That would be mid July, unless they needed to rush them off to Europe.

Frances got a little money each month from him to pay Mr. Snider's rent. The Sniders were always good to pick up things she needed in town. Orvie was walking everywhere and she finally had to put a clothesline on him to keep him from wandering off when she was working in the garden. One day she glanced up to see him playing with a small garden snake. Thereafter, he stayed in the house in his crib when she was in the garden.

She normally walked to church on Sundays, but a time or two Uncle Adren came by to take them in a small buggy. She enjoyed sitting beside him in the pew and listening to him sing. He was the best she'd ever heard. She also got to know one of her aunts better. She still lived at home with Grandpa and Grandma Whitford. They always made it to church but never had much to say. Frances knew her grandpa to be well over 70. Old and worn out, they had experienced a tough life.

It was a Saturday morning in July when a strange car drove up in front of the house. It was the sheriff and he had a message for Frances. Orville had been hurt. He had started home the day before from camp and was hit by a wheel that came off a car along the highway. It had hurt his leg, and he was in a hospital in St. Louis. It wasn't life threatening, but it would be a day or two before he knew when he'd get home. After the sheriff left, Frances rushed over to Mrs. Snider's with the news. John said he'd go to town and make a call or two to see if there was anything that could be done. It was hours before he returned. With the sheriff's help, he had gotten hold of the hospital and found out that the Army doctors had been called in to examine Orville's leg and had not decided what to do yet.

After three days of anxiously waiting for more information, John went back into town for Frances and contacted the hospital again. He came home with the news that Orville's leg had been severely broken below the knee, but the main damage was to the knee itself. They had the leg in a cast and would release him the next day. Orville told them to tell his wife that he had a ride lined up and not to worry. It was after noon the next day when a large car pulled up outside and Orville got out of it. He had a cane and was walking very awkwardly, so Frances helped him into the house. He was exhausted and in some pain, and he lay back on the bed and rested a while before he felt like talking or even holding Orvie.

When he was rested, he said the worse of it was he'd probably never be able to bend his knee again. Because of that, the Army was going to release him. He was trained as a foot soldier and didn't have any talents or education to do anything else, and it was easiest just to send him home. Although his injury wasn't war-related, he thought he might get a small pension for it; but most definitely he was going to collect from the man who owned the car that caused the accident. They had already agreed to pay all medical bills and had offered a $2000.00 settlement if he'd sign a paper. He'd thought it over and decided to do it, and they would get the money in a few days. The doctor had said the cast could probably come off in about eight weeks, but that the knee might need more medical attention because it had been crushed pretty badly. Later, they found out they couldn't fix it, so he decided not to do anymore about it and it would remain stiff the rest of his life.

John came over that next week, and he and Orville had talked for a long time about Orville's future. Later Orville told Frances that John would have to keep the part-time hand that he had hired to replace Orville for the rest of this year, but that maybe they could work out something for next year. Orville had also discussed the little farm they lived on. It wasn't very close to the rest of the Snider land, and was only ten acres surrounded by woods with a stream on the east. Because he was expecting a settlement on his accident, he asked John if he'd consider selling this land to Frances and him. John said he'd talk to his mother, but that it made sense and would certainly help him with his workload.

The money came, and Orville opened an account in Oakland and came home with a plow horse of his own. After the crops were in, Mrs. Snider sold them the farm and the milk cow, and with the money left they bought a regular heating stove and paid off the bed and chest they had bought earlier. The war was over on November 11, 1918, and they were doing pretty good and had a very nice Christmas. Sitting around bothered Orville a lot, but Frances thought that would change when he got busier in the spring.

Orville didn't get his government pension as he thought he might, but they paid him a mustering out pay or settlement for the balance of his enlistment, about $175.00. With that money Orville bought a car. Some of the neighbors wondered how he could drive a car when the house seemed to need so much work. To celebrate they made their first trip that Sunday, first to church and then around the county to see Raymond, Uncle Adren, and some of the people Orville had worked for over the years. Orvie loved riding, and when he wasn't asleep, he stared with big eyes at all there was to see. Later they would regret spending the money on a car, but this day they were having a wonderful time.

With the car came new friendships for Orville. Some of the neighbors who rarely spoke in the past started stopping by, and more and more Orville would be going out in the evening. One day when Orville was in the field, Frances was surprised to find a jug behind the seat of the car with what she took to be whiskey in it. She mentioned it to him, and he just laughed and said he wouldn't try to bring it into the house. He'd keep it in the shed. After that she started noticing and could tell when he was drinking, although she never considered him a drunk. It seemed to make him happier, and things were going along pretty well. She knew that he wasn't going to stop.

In the spring of 1919, Orville plowed the garden first and then set to plowing the ten acres to put in their own first crops. He had bought a single bottom plow, and old Mabel, the horse, pulled it back and forth all day long with Orville walking stiff-legged behind it. He stopped quite often for a rest and a drink. Sometimes his stops were near the shed, and Frances wasn't sure it was always for water. The weather didn't always cooperate, so some days were interrupted and he'd get in the car and leave for a while.

One day he mentioned the money was running low and that it'd be a long time before the crops were ready, so he was trying to make a little extra money. He said he was helping out over at the Stark place. Frances didn't know the Starks but didn't think they were farmers. This new job worried him, and his happier moments appeared to be fewer and farther between. The happier ones were when they were sitting around after supper with their big boy who was now over three years old and growing like a weed.

One day in May they got word that one of the neighbor's sons, which had gotten hurt in Europe during the war, had died in a hospital in the city. Frances baked a pie to take over, and went outside to tell Orville she was going to walk over to take the pie to them. He was in the garden at the time, and she asked him to watch Orvie while she was gone. He said he would. She brought Orvie out to the garden along with the clothesline rope to fasten him, but Orville just waved his hand and said to go on, he'd take care of things.

She went down the road and across the creek that was still a little swollen from the spring rains. There were several people at the neighbors already and they visited for a while before she started back. Walking back, she was enjoying the spring flowers and was feeling good. She hadn't felt this good in a long time. As she came around the corner of the house, Orville was just coming out of the shed and seemed a little uneven in his walk. She looked around for Orvie but didn't see him. She asked Orville where he was. He replied, "He's here somewhere." Orvie wasn't to be seen in the field where the corn was still very small, so she went back to check the house. She was hurrying now and getting more nervous by the minute. No Orvie anywhere and now she was yelling at Orville to quit messing around out there and find him. She looked up and down the road and in the ditches, but he wasn't there. For some reason she started running as fast as she could for the creek bed that bordered the field, all the while yelling at Orville to help her. The weeds along the creek bed had grown pretty high, and she almost stepped off a three-foot drop hidden by the weeds when her eyes caught sight of a little blue shirt lying in the water. She jumped down the ledge and ran to the spot where her little boy had fallen, face down. She felt she was moving in slow motion as she picked him up and looked in his face just as Orville showed up. He wasn't breathing. That was the last she remembered.

Later, Orville revived her with a wet washcloth. When she was fully conscious, she sat up asking for her son, already knowing what she would find. A neighbor pointed to the bedroom where his lifeless form was lying on the bed. She tenderly picked him up and held him to her chest; now fully realizing she had lost the most precious thing in her life. She just held him close and whispered to the lifeless form, "We'll meet on that beautiful shore, my dearest Orvie."

They next few days were a fog as she went through the necessary motions in a lifeless manner. She would pull away when Orville tried to comfort her but it wasn't a conscious thing. As it was, neither of them were comforted. Little Orvie was laid to rest in the Oak Grove Cemetery next to the church. Mom, Raymond, and some others were there, but it was only Mrs. Snider who seemed to truly understand the enormity of her loss, or so she thought. She found out later that her daddy was at the service, too, but didn't try to talk to her because Orville had told him to stay away. No one but Orville and Frances really knew what happened that tragic day, and Frances felt there was nothing to gain by placing blame. She didn't tell what happened, and that knowledge would always remain her secret. Not telling did more than that to Orville. Only time would reveal the cost.

Chapter 6

࣓ঌ

The Difficult Year

Days would pass when just a few necessary words were said between them. When she finally bothered to notice Orville, his beard had grown out and he was as unkempt as the weeds that were taking over the garden and crops. He appeared as though he was doing more drinking than working. She finally got busy in the garden, wanting to spend as much time away from him as she could. Some days she wasn't even sure the cow got milked.

Depression and crying were a daily routine, and her body acted accordingly. Sometimes she would kneel in the garden for an hour at a time, asking for strength. Nothing seemed to be working right. She tried going to church but found she was angry every time she looked out the window and saw the cemetery. The preacher and some of the ladies called on her a couple of times, but she felt her spirit had died, and she was letting her Bible collect dust. For the first time in her life she was truly questioning God. She had hit an all time low.

Despite her lack of appetite and her depression, she noticed signs that she was getting fleshy in the middle. At first she ignored it, and then began remembering that she hadn't had a normal cycle for several months. She had attributed it to her grief, but by the first of September she knew it was more than that. Again, she turned to Mrs. Snider in her time of crisis, and she began telling Frances about the wonderment of life and that it was meant to be to help her through this difficult time. She could tell that she and Orville had grown a part, and her son John had mentioned that he thought Orville was drinking pretty heavily. He suspected Orville was even distilling his own liquor now that the money had run out. With Mrs. Snider's nurturing, she slowly began to recover. She had a new reason to live and it was necessary to eat healthy for her baby. She began to prepare for what lay ahead. If she carried the baby full term, she would be having another January baby.

In late September Orville had gone to town for a few things and was late getting back. He walked in just before dusk with a sack of supplies, and Frances asked him if the car had broken down. He said, "No, I sold it. We needed the money." He seemed sober enough, so she asked him to sit down at the table while she brought his food. While he ate, she told him what was happening. His head sank lower and lower until his nose was almost touching his plate. When she finished, he didn't say anything. Finally he said, "I can't do this again," and pushed his chair back and headed for the door. She heard the shed door close, and it was three days before she saw him sober again. During this time she picked her Bible up again and began to read. She had been neglecting the thing that she needed the most and was just now rediscovering that fact. Slowly her strength returned.

The crops didn't do very well that fall, and there weren't any neighbors coming by wanting Orville to work part time. The car money was about all that was getting them by. Orville had taken to sleeping in the bedroll and didn't bother her, and she cooked for him and didn't bother him. He'd sometimes be gone for a day at a time and he wasn't always drinking, but his moods were dark and she didn't question him. She knew there were times when he had a lot of leg pain, but he didn't say. He always made sure she had plenty of wood, water, and flour, and that the cow got milked before he left on his trips. He'd ride off on old Mabel, and when he came home, he always carried a few supplies. Frances asked him once where he got the money, but he didn't bother saying. After that, she just didn't question him anymore. The neighbor bought their cream and that made them a few cents each week. They had their health and their ten acres. There were a lot of people that didn't have that much, so Frances never complained about her difficult life. She did the best she could with what she had. It took a while, but before long she started back to church on a regular basis. She was going to have another child and it would be brought up right. She was determined that this baby would be loved with all her heart, even though a part of that heart would always be missing Orvie.

She didn't see her momma after the funeral, but sometimes Uncle Adren would bring news to her and carry her news back to Ashmore. For some reason she didn't want to tell her mother about the baby coming, but Uncle Adren noticed and probably had told her. At Christmas Uncle Adren brought a basket of fruits and vegetables, and Mrs. Snider sent used clothing. She got Orvie's baby things out and did what she could to get them ready for the new baby.

She walked to church on pretty days, and once in a while a neighbor would bring her home in a buggy or an automobile. Christmas came and went, and Orville didn't even say anything to her about it, so she didn't mention it either. She just read the Christmas story again in her Bible, and prayed for the baby she was carrying, and wept a little. This had been a painful year.

Beginning in early January, it seemed that Orville was more attentive than usual. He was helping with most of the chores, and it appeared that he was sober when he was home. He kept clean-shaven and made it a point to never be away for too long a period at a time. He even went over to talk to Mrs. Kite; the midwife, and made plans for the delivery. When Frances needed specific things, he even made the trip to town without complaint. Frances appreciated the fact that he was putting his best foot forward as her time drew near.

Frances woke up January 22 with cramps, and knew it wouldn't be long. Orville was ready to go for Mrs. Kite, but she said it would be a while and wanted to wait and make sure it wasn't a false alarm. By noon she was back in bed and in bad pain; but just about the time Frances thought it was time for Orville to go, the pain would subside. This happened time and again over the next twenty-four hours, and Orville was right there doing everything she asked him to do. At about ten o'clock the next evening, the pain began to come and go with some regularity, and she told Orville it was finally time. He was out the door and in less than thirty minutes was back with Mrs. Kite. It was still a while, though, and the baby was born at about four in the morning,

January 24, 1920. The baby was smaller than her first one, but it seemed the delivery was harder. Frances felt a little guilty because she didn't have the same joy that she had with her first one.

The ladies from the church stopped by on a regular basis during the next two weeks, as the weather permitted, and helped her in so many ways. Mrs. Snider and her daughter-in-law came bearing gifts, and she was pleased to see them. But the memory of Orvie still lingered. It was going to take a while for things to feel normal again, if ever. When people asked why she chose the name Leo, she could only say, that's his name. It had just come to her. She didn't even know any Leos.

As she regained her strength, she noticed that Orville returned to some of his old habits. He didn't seem to be drinking as much, but he would be gone for a day at a time and wasn't showing much interest in his baby son. However, she had to admit that he was there this time when she needed him and in time they were living as husband and wife again. No longer sweethearts, but at least looking out for each other's welfare.

These years were prosperous ones for the country, and it did seem like work was available to help the small farmer survive. They didn't gain but they didn't lose. The next year William was born. Two years later Arthur came along and in 1925 Theodore. She had her hands full with four boys and Orville did just enough to feed the family. They fought through illnesses without doctors, and when the cow died they had to take a loan on the property to buy another one to help feed the growing family.

The rest of their family had spread out and lives were changing. Willis graduated from the teacher's college at Charleston. He had a job teaching near there now. Frances' mom and dad also moved to Charleston where they had a larger church, and Evangeline had married a farmer near Windsor. She still saw Uncle Adren from time to time. He had met a young lady at Charleston and they married. He had two children already. He was pretty busy and he didn't get the chance to stop by as often as he once had. She missed him. Raymond was newly wed, also with a son, and they still lived in the tenant house near Ashmore but had greatly improved it. Sally had found a good husband and now had three children. They had moved away from the county.

The heavy drinking was taking its toll on Orville. He looked much older than his twenty-eight years, but she didn't say much about his drinking as she realized that now he did it to kill the constant pain he had in his knee. Even with the kids it was a rare time when he experienced any joy, but he did what he could to provide, and for that she gave him credit.

After William's birth, Frances' faith was fully renewed and she began to enjoy her boys again. She would never forget Orvie, but her boys were a joy to her. They went to church together and had fun and games together as much as time permitted. She did everything with them and she was the one that would boost all four of them up on old Mabel's back for a ride around the yard. At the end of the day she was exhausted when she tucked them in, but it was a sweet exhaustion.

Mrs. Snider's condition troubled her. She was bed-ridden now, and Frances would take the boys over to see her from time to time. She was a sweet lady and always lifted Frances' spirits when Frances' intentions were to make her feel better. She did have a fine son and daughter-in-law to look after her and Frances prayed that the Lord would give her joy and peace to the end.

Chapter 7

❧❧

Beauty and Tragedy

At age twenty-six, Frances was content with what life had dealt her. For one who had been a homely little girl with no self-esteem, she had already lived more life that she thought she would. She had a husband and family, and at one time in her life she didn't think she would ever have succeeded in having that much. Yes, she had hard knocks but she didn't know anyone who hadn't. She had four wonderful sons and didn't expect to get pregnant again. When she did, it was a surprise to her. She carried the baby to term and this time gave birth to a tiny little girl weighing less than five pounds. She even had a doctor this time for the delivery. She couldn't believe how petite and beautiful her baby girl was. Had the Lord saved this special child for her? Uncle Adren suggested the name Ursie after his older sister who had died when she was nine. He said the family had always talked about how strikingly beautiful she was, and little Ursie would certainly be that, too. So Ursie it was. Her momma liked that idea also.

With Orville it was love at first sight. He never showed any of the boys one-tenth of the love and affection he showered on his little girl. It seemed to give him a new reason for living, and he wanted to take her everywhere to show her off. It was a two-way street; from six months on, it was apparent that she was daddy's girl. Frances had never seen him happier, and apparently it even helped him to ignore some of his pain.

Ursie was slow in gaining weight and also rolling over and sitting up. She seemed healthy, and they weren't overly concerned that she was late to crawl. At nine months there were times that she seemed to have a bluish hue to her lips, and they decided to see the doctor in Oakland about it. Oakland had a woman doctor and that was unusual in rural Illinois. After a close examination by the doctor, she said she was concerned that Ursie might have a heart abnormality. In her experience these sometimes took care of themselves; but if it was a hole in the heart or a bad valve, this could be serious. They told her they didn't have the money for a trip to see a specialist in Chicago, so she said to watch and wait for a while. If she seemed to get bluer or had any other difficulties they were to bring her in right away. Orville was beside himself with concern, and Frances tried to be hopeful and encouraging so that he wouldn't get depressed again.

Ursie did walk shortly after a year old, and while she tired easily she was a happy child that her brothers doted on. Leo and Bill went to the Canaan School just up the road, an easy walk, but Art and Ted were with her all day and they played well together. An old box or a can of clothespins gave them hours of entertainment. She was a joy to behold and would always have four brothers who would do anything for her.

Ursie caught colds easily and had a bad one about the time she turned two that really scared her parents. They took her to the doctor and stayed there with her for two days before the doctor let them take her back home. She told them at that time to find a way to get Ursie to a hospital in Chicago to see a specialist as soon as they could work it out. Her size and her overall health just weren't progressing the way it should, and anything, such as the cold could be life threatening.

They had a good crop that year, and Orville had worked around for other farmers. It took all they had just to get through the winter. With five children it was difficult to make ends meet. They discussed it and decided they would have to go to the bank and use the land to get a loan so that they could get Ursie to Chicago. The value of land had increased in the last ten years, and they hoped the bank could give them a big enough loan to get the help for Ursie that she needed. The bank said they would loan up to two thousand, with the land as collateral, and so they took the maximum amount not knowing what to expect.

With the family, it was only logical that both Frances and Orville couldn't go to Chicago with Ursie. Frances wanted to make the trip, but it made more sense that Orville take Ursie and Frances would just have to stay at home with the boys. They both knew that Orville was better equipped to make the trip with their little girl. Dr. Beck made arrangements with a doctor in Chicago, and it was decided to catch the train in Mattoon to go there. It was just after the first of the year in 1930 that they were to leave, and Frances held onto her little girl tighter and for a longer time than ever before. She had even said in her ear, "We'll be together again honey, we'll be together again, don't be afraid." The boys said their good byes. Then Ursie and Orville left for the train, being driven by John Snider in his car.

Orville left her with just enough cash to make it through the month. Arrangements with the pastor at the church had been made so Orville could call him, and he would get the message to Frances. His was the closest telephone. For eight days Frances went through the motions and cared for the boys without hearing a word from Chicago.

Sunday was pretty, so she bundled the boys up and walked the distance to church because she needed some contact with adults, and also she needed to see the preacher. As she went in the front door, he was there to meet her and said, "Frances, how glad I am you could make it. I was heading your way after services if you didn't. I got a call last evening from Orville and he wanted me to give you a message." She began to tremble but managed to say, "Is my baby okay? Did they fix her? Will they be coming home soon?" The preacher held her hand and explained to her that a lot of doctors had looked at Ursie, and they were going to try something new Monday to see if they could help her. Apparently she did have a hole in her heart. They were at the Cook County Hospital in Chicago, and Orville said he'd call as soon as he knew anything else." She didn't hear much of the music and sermon that Sunday. She could only sit in the pew and pray for her little Ursie, so far away and in the hands of strangers.

There was no word Monday, Tuesday, or Wednesday and finally she had to know. Mrs. Edmond, next door, agreed to watch her boys long enough for her to go over and see the preacher again. It had turned off bitter cold. Her coat was bare-thread thin, and by the time she got there she was miserable with the cold. Mrs. Curtis led her into the house and to the stove. Frances apologized for the trouble but said, "Hasn't there been any calls? He said he'd call. My little girl's up there in the hospital and I got to know!" The preacher fully understood but said he hadn't heard anything. Frances said, "Can't we try something? Can't we call the hospital?" The preacher said he would do what he could and went into his study.

His wife had made some hot coffee for Frances and helped her off with her coat. In about ten minutes the preacher came back and said the operators were working to put a call through to the Cook County Hospital and would ring back. Two hours later they still had not called. Finally about three o'clock in the afternoon, the phone rang and he rushed to answer it. He called to Frances to come into his study. "What's the name of Ursie's doctor? They don't know how to get hold of your husband." Frances searched her brain and said, "Dr. Beck sent Orville to see a Dr. Barker." The preacher conveyed this message over the phone, and after a few minutes he scribbled some information on a piece of paper and then hung up. He explained to Frances that Dr. Barker wasn't on staff there, but they had looked up his private office number for them. Frances was beside herself. She needed to know, but it was going to get dark and she had told Mrs. Edmond she wouldn't be gone long. It had already been over three hours. The preacher said he would try and picked up the phone again. He gave the operator the information and was told again that she'd call back if she got through, they were having some bad storms up there. Frances just sat with her face in her hands trembling when he told her he'd give her a ride home. There was no telling how long it would be, and he'd bring any message just as soon as one came in. They picked up the boys on the way home and she struggled with her emotions the whole time she was trying to get them some supper and put them to bed. She wanted to protect them, and she was afraid she wasn't doing a very good job. They asked a lot of questions about Ursie.

The preacher came by Thursday to say the call still wasn't going through. He also stopped by the Sniders to tell them of Frances' predicament, but Mrs. Snider was sick in bed. John said he would look in on Frances to see if he could do anything. Friday morning he came bringing food his wife had prepared. Unknown to Frances, John had also asked the preacher to call Reverend McGrew in Charleston and inform him of the situation.

It was mid-afternoon when the preacher came again. He'd talked to Dr. Barker and found out he had only referred Orville to Cook County and he too didn't know where Orville was or who Ursie's doctors were. The doctor didn't offer any help in contacting the hospital for them. What the preacher didn't tell Frances was that he'd talked to Reverend McGrew and got even less help from him than he had from Dr. Barker. He had said, "She's made her bed, let her lie in it." He was shocked at what he heard and a bit ashamed to call the man Reverend. He had a woman with four small boys with about the least support that any person could have in the time of need. He and his wife prayed long and hard for Frances and her family. When he left Frances huddled in front of the fire, he told her, "I'll keep trying and asking around for ideas on what we can do. Maybe the sheriff's office might know how."

It was Monday when the sheriff talked to the judge at Charleston. He'd told him he couldn't get any cooperation, but that maybe the judge could use his influences. The judge owed the sheriff a couple of favors, so he got busy on the phone. By the afternoon he had news. "I had to go to the top to get to the bottom of this, and the news is bad. The little girl died on the operating table a week ago, and they'd been trying to contact the father ever since to ask what to do with the body." This was the news the sheriff didn't want to deliver. He stopped by the Oak Grove Church to get the Reverend Curtis. They made the trip to see Frances together. Mrs. Curtis called the ladies in the church and they were close behind. They'd all be needed.

The next few days were totally lost to Frances. The burden fell on Reverend Curtis to handle much of the details plus to make sure the ladies of the church saw to it the boys were well cared for. Little Ursie was brought home on a train from Chicago in a small box, and the little body could not be viewed. There wasn't a person in Canaan who did not know of Frances' loss, and they did all they could do to ease her burden. Still there was no word from Orville.

Her family, Raymond, and all the neighbors were at the Oak Grove service as Ursie was laid to rest. The Reverend McGrew was not at the burial. The sheriff was pursuing efforts to trace Orville but wasn't having any luck so far.   Raymond had offered to do what he could but didn't have any money to go to Chicago.   The sheriff assured him that going to Chicago without a lead would be fruitless.   Raymond's wife offered to keep the boys a few days until Frances got back on her feet.   Frances told the preacher, "I don't know what I'm going to do. My money will run out soon and the bank has already been around. They heard Orville was missing and wanted to see what arrangements were being made to make the loan payments. I thought it was awfully soon, but rumors are that the banks are beginning to hurt too with the business world collapsing this past fall. I didn't think banks could go broke, but, they sure are in a hurry to hear from Orville." The Reverend passed this conversation on to John Snider.

Frances did get her boys back home the following week. She needed them badly now and wanted them near. Her momma had given her five dollars and someone had chipped in for the burial expenses. She was skimping on everything to try and get through the winter. The neighbors were generous in bringing in food for over a month.

Mrs. Snider died in March, and Frances had a chance to see her once more before she died. She sat next to her bed and held the lady who had been more of a mother to her than her own, and prayed and wept over her. Mrs. Snider recognized her and smiled. As she left to go home, she hugged Mrs. Snider and whispered in her ear, "If we never meet again this side of heaven, we'll meet on that beautiful shore." Two days later she passed to go on to be with her loving husband.

It was early spring when it became obvious to Frances that once again she was pregnant. She had suspected it for two months and prayed it wasn't true, but there was no denying it anymore. She didn't tell anyone, not even the kids. No husband, no money, and all too soon no home, because the bank had started foreclosure proceedings for their $2000.00. The situation couldn't have been more hopeless. John had made one payment to the bank that had bought her a little time, but she couldn't let him do that anymore. Things were getting tough all over and he needed his money for seed. The church had taken up a couple of special collections in her behalf, but the second was a lot smaller than the first, and it became apparent that people just couldn't help much more.

Unknown to Frances, things were happening in Charleston that involved her parents. When the sheriff got the judge's support to help Frances, he shared as much as he knew about Frances and how her father had disowned her. To the judge's surprise, the father was the Reverend William McGrew, who had one of the larger congregations in Charleston. He began to ask around among different friends in Ashmore and the county and got the story, not necessarily accurate, of the happenings over the last dozen or so years. It seemed to the judge that his treatment of his daughter had been rather harsh and not very becoming for a man of the cloth. He shared his opinion with several influential people, and as word spread the attendance at Reverend McGrew's church began to fall. Before long the elders of the church called on the Reverend and asked for his resignation. His reputation was hurting the church. Rev. McGrew began to look around but found that no one was looking for a preacher whose character had been questioned. The lack of forgiveness is not a trait that most Christians can understand, so in his middle fifties he was out of a job and was asked to vacate the parsonage. He found a small two-room house that he could afford to rent and moved his wife there. Although not well, his wife Mary was soon taking in washing and ironing to stretch what little savings they had.

Also unknown to Frances was the fact that Mr. Knight, known to friends as Big Jess, who lived on the Oakland Ashmore road had lost his wife in February, leaving him with three sons at home to raise. He had a sizeable farm and apparently didn't lack for money, but needed someone to cook for him and the boys and take care of the house. The Reverend Curtis knew of the job and approached Frances about it the first of May. Although he suspected she was pregnant, she above anyone he knew truly needed a job. He didn't think it would do any harm for him to talk to Big Jess for her, if she was interested. She was in such desperate straits. Believing the bank would have her home soon, she asked the Reverend to check into it for her.

Later he came back and said Mr. Knight was looking for a housekeeper who could live in and wasn't really interested in a lady with four kids. That was when the preacher suggested she might have to get some county help for the boys if there wasn't family to help out. At first she resisted, but after receiving a legal eviction notice delivered by the sheriff she had to think some more about it. She was at rock bottom and asked the preacher to call her mother and fill her in to see if she had any ideas to help her. She really needed to sit down with her but that just wasn't feasible at the time. She sat in the study with him as he made the call. He contacted the church in Charleston, although he wasn't looking forward to talking to the Reverend McGrew again. He asked for the Reverend and listened while someone explained to him the situation. He said thank you and hung up turning to Frances. "You're father isn't the pastor there anymore. He was asked to leave last month and as far as the lady on the phone knows, he's still living in Charleston." She was stunned at this news and could only sit there speechless. She thought to herself, "I think this is the straw that broke the camel's back."

She thought of Raymond and couldn't see how he could be any help. She thought of Uncle Adren but knew he had his hands full. Uncle Adren had four children and another was expected soon. Times were rough over there too, and she couldn't think of one person who could or would help her out of the jam.

After a couple of sleepless nights, she finally came to a conclusion. With a surge of energy she walked over to the church and asked Reverend Curtis if he had time to take her over to see Mr. Knight. She wanted to talk to him. He said, "Let's go." And down the road they went. As they pulled up to the house Big Jess and a couple of the smaller kids came out the door. The Reverend said, "Jess, this is the woman I talked to you about. The one that could do the job you need done. She's had lots of experience with children and is a good Christian lady." Big Jess looked at her, and it was hard to tell what he was thinking. Frances spoke up uncharacteristically for her and said, "Mr. Knight, I heard about your loss and am sorry. I know how you feel about my kids, but they're good minding boys and wouldn't interfere with my work." She was about to say something else when Big Jess raised his hand and said, "I don't have anything against kids but there just isn't room for them here. Beside that, is there something I should know about your condition? That's just a lot to ask for and I'm sorry, but I can't start something that don't have much chance to work." Her chin fell to her chest and tears shown in her eyes. The Reverend said, "I understand Jess, and I thank you for talking to Frances. We'll be going now." As they turned to walk away,

Big Jess cleared his voice and said, "I know the predicament you're in, Mrs. Trapp. Maybe if you could place the kids in the county home for a while, you could work until your time comes. I don't have any other prospects anyhow, and I might help with the county commissioner in finding a place for the boys." Frances almost said "No, thanks", but hesitated and said, "I'll think it over."

By the following morning she knew what she had to do and sat down with the older boys to try to explain it. It would only be for a little while, but it'd be a big help to her if the boys could go live in the children's home for a while until they got back on their feet or until their dad showed up, it might not be long at all. They cried and hugged her neck, but there wasn't anything else she could do. The bank was forcing her to vacate the house and she had to protect her boys.

Big Jess had immediate misgivings after he made his offer, but when the Reverend showed up the next day with her acceptance, he just couldn't go back on his word. It would only be for three or four months at most probably, and it would give him help until someone else came along. And besides, that little woman had more troubles than she deserved.

John Snider had told Frances he'd gladly store her furniture for her until she needed it. Things were falling into place when the sheriff and the Reverend got the boys accepted at the home in Charleston. She signed the papers for the county and assured them that it would only be temporary. When the sheriff picked up the boys, she hugged each and assured them she loved them with all her heart. She pulled Leo aside and asked him to look after the younger ones. "I'm proud of you," she said as she gave him a special hug. Just after they left, the mail carrier came by, catching Frances still in the yard and handed her an envelope. They didn't even have a mailbox because they'd never had mail. The outside of the envelope was addressed to Orville Trapp. Up in the corner it said Cook County Hospital, Chicago, Illinois. Her hands trembled as she opened the letter. Inside was a bill. It read, "For medical services rendered, $1800.00. Received on account, $1400.00, Balance due, $400.00. Balance overdue. Please pay." She could only stare at the paper she held in her hand. She thought, "Orville, where are you and what are you doing? Don't you know you're needed here? Your family is tearing apart."

47

At that exact moment in time, Orville Trapp was sitting in a filthy prison cell near Gary, Indiana. He remembered he still had two hundred dollars in his pocket when Ursie had died. He hadn't given that to the doctors yet, but it disappeared in the drunken haze that followed. When he sobered up, he was in a jail cell someplace in northern Indiana, penniless and accused of breaking and entering. They told him it was the middle of February and he'd been caught trying to sell gold plated candlesticks taken from some doctor's house. He was picked up without any thing in his possession and wouldn't cooperate with the police, refusing to give his name or home address. He had several injuries to the scalp and back that needed medical treatment, some of which were pretty badly infected. The toes on his bad leg had been frost bitten and were painful, but with treatment they were saved. He refused to give his name because his shame and failure was more than he could face the people back home with. In the end, he was tried and convicted as a John Doe and given fifteen months in prison for the theft. Now that he had gotten over withdrawal from alcohol, he recognized that being arrested probably saved his life. If it had not been for that, he probably would have been found frozen in some field somewhere. He decided that he'd serve his time, and then return home to see if there was any future there for him. After losing Ursie, he really didn't much care one way or another. He had been the reason Orvie died, and now he had stood by and watched doctors fail to save the one bright light of his life. The memories haunted him and only added to his misery. The prison was like a pigsty and he lived in filth, but he knew he deserved all of this and more.

Chapter 8

❧ ❧

The Long Wait

The first month at the Knight's house went well. Frances tried to treat the Knight boys like she would have her own, and they seemed to respond to it. James was the oldest with Burdette and Dan following. Dan was only five. Frances had her own room off the kitchen, and while it wasn't large, it had room for a small bed and a chest. That was plenty of room for what she had. She was up at daybreak and normally was back in her room by eight at night. Big Jess' instructions were short and to the point, and he didn't hesitate to tell her if she was doing anything wrong or something he didn't like. More than once that first month, he had said, "Don't be babying those boys. They've got to grow up sometime." He himself didn't show very much outward affection to his boys, and although he treated them fairly, he struck her as a man who didn't want anything to get to close to him.

They liked her cooking and the house was always clean. Fortunately for her the pregnancy went well and not once did she have to ask for any special consideration. She expected the baby the first of September, and with any luck she thought she could work within a week of that. She didn't want to give Big Jess any reason to regret giving her this chance.

Big Jess had two older children, both grown and married. They never visited, but the boys would talk about them once in a while. The

49

older sister had gone to Florida with her husband and the boys talked about her being rich. She sent them gifts but hadn't visited them recently. There was an absence of personal things such as pictures around the house, so Frances couldn't relate to Big Jess' daughters or his deceased wife. Frances thought this unusual. Big Jess let the boys go to church with Frances on Sundays. He never went, but he kept his wife's old Bible out on the parlor table. She even saw him reading it on a regular basis. Jim, the oldest of the three, was a calm mature boy for his age. The younger two were typical boys with mischievous ways.

About the middle of July, Frances approached the preacher at church and asked if he could check up on the boys. Later on he said he had made a call and they were adjusting well, but if she could get away he would drive her over one day for a visit. Visitation was very limited, but he didn't think one this soon would be any problem. Soon after he took her to the county children's home to see her sons. It was a brick two-story building and housed about eighteen children. The kids were outside in the heat of the day when they drove up, and the boys spotted Frances right away and ran over to her. Amid laughter and tears they went over under the shade tree where they visited an hour together. She thought they all looked well, and they told her they were treated well. Those that didn't behave got strapped pretty often.

She examined each boy carefully, preserving the image in her mind to fill the days and weeks ahead. With the exception of William, they were all short for their age and had the big gap in their front teeth like her. William was taller and dark like his dad with black hair and gray eyes. He had already passed up Leo in height. The youngest, Ted, was the first to ask if she'd come to take them home. She wrapped him in her arms and sobbed as she explained to all of them that their daddy still wasn't home and that it might take awhile longer before she could get them home. One other thing she said, "As you can see, another baby is on the way but one day we'll all be together as a family." Art ask if she would name the baby Eddie. Eddie was his best friend here, and their cots were close together and he really liked him. His mother said, "Eddie or Edward sounded like a fine name, if it's a boy. You wouldn't want a sister named Eddie would you?" Art said, "Oh, it's a boy alright." What a prophet he turned out to be. Leaving them wasn't any easier than the first time, but she was happy that they were well cared for.

Mrs. Kite was much older than she was when she brought Orvie into the world, but she still had all of Frances' confidence. She trusted her more than she did the doctor who had delivered Ursie. Eddie was born in her little room off the kitchen with Big Jess, the boys, and Reverend and Mrs. Curtis in the parlor. The delivery was much easier than most of the others because the baby was even smaller than Ursie. The first time Frances held the baby, she thought, "This must have been what I looked like as a baby, except maybe not quite so poorly." The big mouth and the pug nose were already there and she thought to herself, "I hope it's easier getting by in this world for a homely boy than it is for a homely girl."

Within a week Frances was at full strength again around the house. Other than asking her if she needed anything, Big Jess made no comment about her job status or the future. The baby didn't sleep through the nights, but back in her little room she guessed he wasn't disturbing anybody. It didn't interfere with her job, even though she was constantly tired and had developed a cough. She suppressed it pretty much when anyone was around, but sometimes when it was just she and Eddie at home, it was hard to control. Eddie wasn't gaining as he should, and she felt maybe the cough was the cause of his not nursing properly. She finally resorted to weaning him early in order to get him adequately fed.

In early November she caught a terrible cold due to her run-down condition, and at times breathing became very difficult. She tried all the home remedies when Big Jess wasn't around, but one day he came to her and said his son Jim thought she was really sick. The boys were worried about her. It wasn't long before she couldn't get the work done and the coughing was day and night. Not a deep cough but a raspy breathless cough that could go on for ten minutes at a time, leaving her weak, shaken, and breathless. One day when she couldn't make it to the kitchen, Big Jess wrapped her up and took her into Oakland to see Dr. Beck. After examining her, the doctor said it was more than a cold and wanted to know if she was spitting up any blood. Frances said that most of the time it was more like dry heaves, but no blood. She ruled out tuberculosis, but said she was stumped and suggested that Frances needed to go to a hospital for some tests. Frances looked at Big Jess and just knew she could kiss her job goodbye. She'd never witnessed much compassion in him, but he surprised her when he told Dr. Beck, "I'll get her to Charleston right away. We'll find out what's wrong."

After an examination by the doctor on staff, the hospital administration reluctantly admitted her knowing that they'd be lucky to collect a cent. The days stretched into weeks, and after the first of the year the doctors concluded they just couldn't diagnose what the ailment was. She was getting worse by the day. They were keeping her alive with oxygen but finally had to sit down with her and explain that they didn't have the answer. They didn't tell her that they were limited in what they could do because she was a charity case. They also didn't tell her that they didn't give her much chance of living. The doctors did explain this to her pastor and Mr. Knight, because she didn't have any next of kin around at that time. Soon afterward Reverend Curtis showed up with a gentleman who he introduced to Frances as Mr. Kirkley from the county. He wanted to discuss the boys' future. Mr. Kirkley told Frances she had some nice acting boys and he thought they'd have an excellent chance for adoption, but there was one problem. If Frances passed, the County would be legally bound to wait for the father and couldn't let the boys be adopted. He said, "The Reverend has explained the family situation and the fact that there is no family to take them in. I strongly urge you to sign a release for their adoption so we can overcome this missing father problem." Gasping for air, Frances' eyes turned to her preacher, who only nodded his head and said, "That's the right thing to do." She knew she was dying, but this was the first time she'd been confronted with the knowledge. She wept as she thought of her children and what their future held. She whispered out loud, saying, "If I do this, they have to all go as a family." Mr. Kirkley spread out a document before her and, with tears streaming, she signed her name. "Please let me see them one more time before it's too late." Reverend Curtis said he'd make sure that was done.

Later that day he brought in the two youngest, Ted and Art. They huddled over their mother, crying for her. As they did she said in a weak, raspy voice, "If we never meet again this side of heaven, we'll meet on that beautiful shore." The exertion and emotion was too much and it was two days before she was strong enough to see William. Like the others, she repeated the same words to him. When she asked for Leo, the preacher said Leo had been gone that morning, but that he'd bring him the first chance he got. The next day Frances became unconscious, and was in and out of consciousness over the next week.

When she woke up enough to see, there was an old gray man standing over her bed weeping. "Who are you?" she asked, knowing as she said it that she was looking at her father for the first time in fifteen years. He sank beside her bed on his knees and asked her forgiveness over and over. He'd been proud and arrogant and oh so wrong for so long. It had been he and his wife keeping little Eddie for her that finally gave him the courage to come and see her. He wanted to pray for her. She said in a small, raspy voice, "Thank you for taking care of Eddie. Can he stay with you when I'm gone?" Her father clasped her hands and said, "Forever." With a low voice growing stronger as he prayed over Frances, he asked God to heal this woman, his daughter whom he had never given a chance for a real life. It was he and not she who deserved punishment and he appealed to Jesus for intervention on her behalf. The nurse who thought Frances needed her rest now interrupted him in his prayers. As he left, Frances slipped back into a coma.

The nurses checked her pulse and made sure she was getting liquid intravenously several times daily. Among the staff they talked about how long the feeding and oxygen would continue before she was removed from them and allowed to die. The administration certainly needed the bed but was reluctant to get the court order to do so. This was a small town hospital, and this just didn't happen very often. They did move her out of the main stream and checked her less frequently as time went on.

About a month later, the night nurse noticed on the charts that she hadn't been checked all day and thought there should be at least one entry for the day. As she was taking Frances' pulse, she was surprised how firm it was and looked at the patient only to see the patient staring at her. It startled her to the point that she stumbled over the bedside chair and fell bruising her hip. Getting up she checked Frances again and talked to her. Although the eyelids fluttered, she didn't get any other response. At that hour of the night there wasn't a doctor in the hospital. She brought the relief nurse up to date and thought the morning would be soon enough for the doctor to look at her.

The day shift got pretty excited, and a number of doctors made a visit to the room to see the patient. The doctor told the nurse in charge to get hold of the Reverend McGrew and tell him about the change. While it may not last, he was sure they'd want to know. He just shook his head as he considered the possibilities. The woman he'd given up on, and to whom he had hinted that she get her affairs in order, just might live. It would be a miraculous recovery. When Frances' parents heard the word, they certainly thought so.

By noon Frances was fully conscious, but any attempt to talk resulted in unintelligible noises and facial contortions. Thing were not any better the following day, and the doctors could only relate it to the way stroke victims responded. Her vitals continued to get better, and on the third day they were feeding her a soft diet. It soon became apparent that they would have to work with her, much like a stroke victim, on speech and swallowing. The administration, anxious to minimize their costs on a patient that they had very little chance of collecting from, insisted that she no longer needed full-time nursing care and that other accommodations be made. The Reverend and Mrs. McGrew stepped in immediately and moved her to their home, where her mother could give her the personal care she needed.

Mr. Kirkley had some prospects for the boys even before Frances had gotten sick. There wasn't a surplus of children available for adoption at that time, and several couples had contacted the county to inquire of the availability of children. The desired children were those between the ages of one and ten. He had discouraged more than one prospect with the explanation that while those boys were wards of the county; they just weren't up for adoption. As soon as he had the release signed by Mrs. Trapp, he began to explore the possibilities. There were good prospects. Because of Mrs. Trapp's condition, he felt good that he had an opportunity to find them a real home instead of them living is this institution until they were grown. Also, as a practical matter, it would open up four beds for others in need.

It bothered him a little that on her deathbed Mrs. Trapp had indicated she wanted the boys to be adopted together, but there wasn't anyway he could have explained to the dying woman that this wasn't likely to happen. He had one couple take two children of the same family once, but four just wasn't likely to happen. When the Reverend Curtis had come by a day or two later to take the oldest boy to see his mother for the last time, he'd already sent him for a trial visit with a nice older couple from out of town. After a week he wasn't back, so the chances looked pretty good for him. Within five days he had placed the other three boys in three different locations. The potential adoptive parents all had impressive backgrounds. Unless he was mistaken, the county home had seen the last of these boys. He felt like he had done them and their mother a big service.

It was quite a surprise when a few weeks later the Reverend Curtis had showed up with the news that Mrs. Trapp would likely survive. She wasn't in very good shape and possibly would never be normal again. Rev. Curtis thought she might want to rethink the decision she'd made when the doctors told her she was dying. Mr. Kirkley had mixed feelings about this but conceded that was definitely a possibility. Even if she recovered, what was the likelihood that she could care for the boys? And if she couldn't work, there wasn't even the possibility of her being able to reclaim them from the county. Without giving him any details, he told the Reverend how fortunate he was to have found what appeared to be permanent homes for the boys. The Reverend said, "I see your point, but it sure puts me in a real moral dilemma if she decides she wants to tear the papers up." There weren't any immediate answers to the problem. They'd just have to see how things played out.

Frances was recovering slowly at her parent's house, and it obviously was a great joy to her to have Eddie with her. He was the medicine the medical experts couldn't provide. She was a little girl again, back in her parent's care, but this time it was different. Her father was always around and his tender loving care of both her and Eddie slowly washed away most of the bad memories of the past. She asked about the boys, but didn't want them to see her in her present state. Her speech was badly slurred, and she still was unable to walk on her own or take care of her personal needs. But she could see progress every week.

Reverend McGrew fielded her questions about the boys by just saying, "They're just fine," but he was in fact talking to Mr. Kirkley almost daily and knew the boys were gone. Although he pleaded for their return, he knew the county was right about Frances' ability to raise them alone, and he knew that with his age and health he really couldn't offer any other solution. He had talked to Willis and the others, and they couldn't take on more responsibility either. For them to spend another ten years in institutions was not an acceptable alternative for his daughter's children, even though they were virtual strangers to him. He talked it over with his wife, and after much prayer they agreed it wouldn't serve any purpose to tell Frances about this until she was stable enough physically and mentally to make the right decisions. Meanwhile, he would continue to appeal to the county to wait before finalizing anything.

The county didn't wait. Within four months of their placement, with four separate couples, the adoptions were finalized and the court had the records sealed forever. The judge who had helped ruin the career of the Reverend McGrew made the final decisions. He remembered the family history, and the Reverend's appeal to him to wait fell on deaf ears.

As Frances began to feel better and she could speak more clearly, she wanted very much to see the boys. The parents stalled as long as they could, but finally when they thought she was well enough to cope with the information, they had to tell her. Her parents feared what the devastating facts would do. This news might finish the job that the disease hadn't done. Frances went to bed and they couldn't persuade her to eat for two days. She had lost her will to live until little Eddie, now toddling around the home, started tugging at her arm and crying for attention. Slowly this helped to pull her through. Regaining her health was definitely set back, but by Christmas she had recovered most of her speech and again had control of her bodily functions. Physically she knew she'd recover, but emotionally she wasn't sure she ever would. All that could go wrong that year had gone wrong, but her saving grace was little Eddie to care for. God knew what he was doing.

Frances' presence, while contributing to a new spirit of family with her parents, was also a burden to their health and finances. Her father was trying to find day work, which was mainly manual labor. That was very scarce in 1931 as the economy of the country was further deteriorating. Even when he found work, his body was not equipped to tolerate much of it. Manual labor had just not been his life. Frances knew there were days when a kind neighbor or a friend managed to put food on their table. She knew she had to relieve their burden somehow. They had done so much for her but she had things she needed to do.

She hadn't seen her preacher for about three months when he stopped in after the first of the year. When questioned, he confirmed the status of the boys. Although he thought it was tragic, he also had to be practical and try to get her to consider that this possibly was God's will. Perhaps in years to come she would see how something good could come from it. He was surprised at the progress she had made. When she shared with him the burden she had been to her parents, he thought of something he'd do when he got back home. Reverend Curtis had become better acquainted with the Reverend McGrew and recognized that more than one miracle had happened in the Frances' life. Along with the tragedy of losing her sons, probably forever, there had been an intervention in her health problems. This father and daughter who had been separated so long were now reunited. Along with the bad, some good had come.

Frances cried herself to sleep more than once on her cot. As she lay in bed with little Eddie on a pallet on the floor beside her, each night was spent wondering where her children were, were they well, and would she ever see them again. She hadn't even gotten to say goodbye to Leo, and she wondered if he hated her for abandoning him. She knew her life would never be whole again unless she found them. First she lost Orvie, then Ursie, and now the boys. Orville was gone, too, but she'd lost a big part of him when Orvie had drowned. Because of the grief, the guilt, and the liquor, their marriage had just been a shell for the family to exist in and not the glue it needed to truly hold it together. He'd proven that by not coming home.

She was fighting the March winds that were trying to whip the bedclothes out of her hands at the clothesline. She couldn't believe the number of sheets and blankets that her mother took in every week for laundering. Her concentration covered up the closing of the car door behind her and the first she knew of his presence was when Big Jess said, "Are you sure your well enough to be fighting this cold wind?" She jerked around, and there was the man who had saved her more than once. The man she always considered remote, first gave her work, and then got her to the hospital to help her get well. She was happy to see him.

But when she spoke all she could say was, "What are you doing here?" He said, "It's cold standing here, any chance of getting a cup of coffee?" He followed her inside, and she introduced him to her dad. She found some leftover coffee and placed it in front of him at the table, and apologized for not having any pie. He and the Reverend were making small talk about the weather and the failure of so many banks when she set down with them. Frances said, "How are the boys? Have they been going to church?" Jess said they did most of the time, but they'd mentioned more than once they missed Frances' cooking. She laughed at this news and had a good feeling because Big Jess had taken time to come by. "In fact," Jess said, "I'm here because I'm still trying to find a suitable replacement for you. Do you want a job?" She was surprised and said, "Do you mean you've spent all this time without help?" He told her he'd had replacements but none that lasted. About that time little Eddie toddled up to the table and looked at the big stranger sitting there. Big Jess looked at him for a moment and said, "He's not very big, I think we can find room for him, too." Frances' heart was filled with gratitude and he made arrangements to pick her up at the end of the week. Her dad had been quiet through all of this. When Big Jess got up to leave, the Reverend McGrew followed him outside, shook his hand, and thanked him for his kindness to someone who hadn't had enough kindness in her life.

Chapter 9

❧❦

Long Road Back

Prison life had been tough on Orville. Daily they were trucked out to do roadwork on government land, and he was doing more hard labor now than he had done since injuring the knee. Unknown to him, the judge who sentenced him had sent a note to the warden telling him to find out this John Doe's name. The warden understood what the judge meant, and he did have ways of encouraging people to talk.

After about thirty days the guards escorted Orville to the warden's office. The warden said, "Inmate, you're here for more than a year, and we can make it hard or harder. Your time can be longer if you don't cooperate and do your job. If you give us trouble, you'll be sorry. You'd best learn that this is a different life now, and you will obey the guards. You can start by giving me your proper name now." Orville glanced at the guards on either side and finally said, "I don't mean any disrespect sir. I just don't want to shame my family." The warden said, "As far as we know, you might be wanted for murder in thirty states and I guarantee you'll never get out of here until we can check you out. Think about that."

Orville was led back to his cell and wasn't sure of what else he could have done. In the next couple of days the cellblock guard would ask him when he passed, "Do you have anything for me John Doe?" It was soon after that he noticed he was consistently getting some of the dirtiest and most disgusting work. When the grease pits in the kitchen were stopped up, he got the job of trying to clean them out. Sewage stoppages and any dirty duty that came along fell to him in addition to the daily roadwork. This went on month after month and then one day he was put in the hole, solitary confinement, for mentioning that he thought they could pass this dirty duty around a little.

He learned not to complain, although others did and weren't treated as harshly. Even during the seven days in solitary, the guard bringing him bread and water would ask, "Do you have anything for me Mr. Doe?" Out in the exercise area later, one guy began to harass him. It would have been easy to respond, but that would surely have meant more solitary time. So all he could do was turn and walk away with the jeers of other inmates in his ear. He was sure the guards had put the guy up to it.

For about nine months, he was constantly on edge and the pressure was building to where he really feared that he might try something drastic in a moment of utter desperation. He was again summoned to the warden's office, and this time the man put it on the line. "Either we know who you are, or you're staying. Your guard said you threatened him and that's worth at least a ninety-day extension." Orville stood with his head bowed and knew it was no contest; he'd have to tell. The warden said, "You're time would have been easier if you'd wised up earlier." The next three months were considerably easier, and even some of the guards spoke to him at times like he was a real person.

Those last weeks before his release from prison, Orville had started writing several letters to both his wife and brother, but he never got them finished. What could he say that would mean anything? It seemed that every time something really important was involved, he had failed miserably. That's why he had always admired his younger brother Raymond who, although younger, had always been reliable in finishing the task at hand. That was his mother's trait; unfortunately, he'd developed more of his father's characteristics. In the end the letters didn't get sent, and when he walked out of the gate of the prison that May morning, he was still at a loss of what to do. All he had were the clothes on his back and five dollars the State of Indiana had given him. He did realize what he would have done a year ago. But at least time had cured that problem. He was over drink, and his intent was to never

60

touch another drop for as long as he lived. He found himself following the tracks, and before long a slow freight gave him an opportunity to ride. It was going south at least.

The call had come in from Indiana to Sheriff Sizemore. The caller was an investigator for the Indiana State Police, wanting to know if there were any wants or warrants on an Orville Trapp of Coles County, Illinois. Sheriff Sizemore told them that Orville had been missing since late January, of 1930, but there were no arrest warrants. They informed the sheriff that Orville Trapp was up for release from the Indiana State Penitentiary on May 14, 1931. That was one mystery solved for the sheriff, and he made a call to the Reverend Curtis to inform him of the news.

Chapter 10

❧❦

Picking Up the Pieces

When Reverend Curtis got the news regarding Orville, he wasn't sure what he should do. He knew Frances was in no shape to handle this type of news. She was struggling to get her own health back. He decided to talk to the Reverend McGrew and get his opinion about what should be done. After all, he was the next of kin. By mutual agreement they decided to wait for a better time to tell Frances about where Orville was and why. The weeks turned into months without further information about Orville. They waited until nearly Christmas when she was doing better before they broke the news to her. She took it without much reaction and said, "If he hasn't made it home in six months, there is no reason to expect him, and I don't. It's too late now for him to be of any help."

Frances and Eddie had a daily routine, although not a day passed without her having a sense of loss so strong that she had to find her private space and cry. She was happy to have the work. The contact and relationship with Big Jess' boys definitely helped, but in the quiet moments the faces of her boys haunted her. At night, when she was totally exhausted, she could finally find relief in sleep.

She had two visits with her parents that summer and time was healing old wounds. Eddie had become such a joy for them. Although working hard, their health had seemed better. Uncle Adren dropped in from time to time, and he and Big Jess appeared to hit it off. Despite the difference in their ages, he and Jess had a lot in common. Frances had never seen Big Jess respond to any other person quite the way he did to Adren. Adren, on the other hand, never met a stranger and with his friendliness strangers didn't stay strangers very long.

Things were pretty tough over Adren's way as Grandma and Grandpa Whitford had both died in the past year or two. Her Uncle Adren and his family had moved in with them the last few years to help take care of them. It was a difficult time and Adren had suffered with the loss. On one visit he had brought his oldest son Franklin with him. It was clear that this young man was the apple of his father's eye and a chip off the old block. He was nine or ten and seemed to get along fine with James, but didn't have much in common with the rowdier younger boys. Frances thought he would make a handsome man.

That winter Frances was leaving church services on Sunday when a car pulled up in front of her, and Raymond got out. Raymond didn't attend church at Oak Grove, and Frances wasn't sure whether he went to church at all. She was happy to see him and told him so. He'd always treated her with respect and had always been nice to her children. He said he'd like to talk to her if she had the time, and then he could take her where she was going. She had the boys get into the back seat and got up front with Raymond. She told him how to get to Big Jess's and he started slowly in that direction, asking about her health and sharing about his family. He'd gotten some kind of job with the county having to do with agriculture and had a little home over in the Yellowhammer school district with his wife and two children. He felt lucky to have a job.

He turned up the lane at Big Jess' and stopped before he got back to the house. He turned off the motor and looked over at Frances. "I received a letter from Orville," he said. That caught her off guard a little, but she turned and asked Jim if he'd go ahead and take Eddie on home. After the boys got out, Raymond began by saying the letter had arrived the past week. Orville had been somewhere in Southern Tennessee and apparently was moving around a lot by hitching rides on freight trains. The letter explained to Raymond what had happened and where he had been. It said how ashamed he was, but that he was sober and was still trying to get enough courage to come home. Work was scarce and he'd been going from place to place when he heard rumors of work with the hope of getting some money so he could come home. He made no excuses, but just wanted Raymond to know that he knew how badly he had messed up and that someday he hoped to make amends. He didn't expect forgiveness or even understanding, but he was going to do something. "He hoped and, yes, even prayed that you and the boys were okay," Raymond said. There was no return address to write to because he didn't know where he would be the following week. Frances heard all of this with bowed head and tears slowly falling down her cheeks. Had it been only fifteen years since she had first loved that man? It seemed longer. When Raymond fell silent, she patted him on the arm, said thank you, and got out. She had dinner to prepare.

In 1933 the small farmers were feeling the strain of the depression that controlled the country. Many depended on crop loans to get seed money to plant the fields in the spring. With so many banks failing, the loans were hard to come by. When the small farmer couldn't get the seed money, or if the crop failed, it was those banks and those individuals that did have money that got land at bargain prices. Farmers were forced into liquidation of land to survive, or in most cases banks foreclosed on loans. Several neighbors in Canaan and Yellowhammer had already met this fate. Unless something changed, more small farmers would lose their land in the future. Fortunately Big Jess had always been suspicious of the banks, and he believed in self-sufficiency. He owned his stock and his seed, and wasn't dependent on anyone else. Times were tough, but the Knight family had enough to survive and they shared it with their housekeeper and her small son.

In the fall, Frances had an opportunity to go to Charleston to visit for a couple of days, and while she was there took the time to call on Mr. Kirkley at the children's home. She did not expect to get her boys back, but she thought maybe he had information of their welfare. He was most sincere to her, and explained that all contacts had been closed with the adoptive parents. He did not have any information on the boys, nor would he ever. There was no reason they would ever communicate with him again. It was all out of his hands. In her heart, as much as she'd tried to forgive, she still held a resentment that the boys had been split up by Mr. Kirkley. She was pressing the issue of the boys with him when he finally said, "Let me show you something." Frances followed him into the dormitory rooms of the home where there were more than forty cots where eighteen used to be. Bad times had created more need. He explained to her that had her boys remained, the living conditions would not be as good as they first experienced. Also, had she not survived and the boys were still here, the opportunity for permanent homes would have been reduced significantly. Not only were there more available children now, but there are fewer people looking to expand their families in hard times. He then asked Frances to take a short ride with him out to the County Farm, which was called by most people, the poor farm. He stopped the auto on the road by the recently built wooden structures, and again said the population here had tripled and the available money had to be stretched much further. The dollars to care for the young and old were less than two years ago, even though the need was greater. Staff was being laid off so that they would have money to buy food. Frances rode quietly back to town and, as he dropped her off near her parents' house, she said, "Thank you, sir, for taking your important time to show me these things. I'll not be bothering you again."

1933, 1934, and 1935 were much the same in rural Illinois and more and more parts of the economy sank into economic ruin. Some farmers plowed their crops into the ground because they couldn't harvest them for what the market would pay them. Stories were that the government was buying beef and slaughtering it rather than give it to the needy. Closer to home, in late 1935 the bank foreclosed on Uncle Adren's land, and he had to move his family to Canaan to sharecrop for another farmer. Frances saw very little of him although he was less than three miles away. It appeared that the whole nation was suffering.

Five different times Raymond had shared news with her about Orville, and on two occasions he had sent money to pass on to Frances. It wasn't much, but Frances tucked it away in a special place. She and Eddie had what they needed. In his last letter he put an address in western Texas where he thought he'd be for at least six months. He had a job where he now had a regular check, and he hoped to start home in about six months. He asked Raymond to write and give him some news. At last maybe he would be able to make some amends. Raymond told Frances that he was writing a letter to Orville and he'd share the address if she wanted it. She said, "No, you can tell him what needs to be told."

The Knight boys were doing well, and James was now in high school in Oakland. He could have quit school but told his dad he didn't want to farm all his life. Big Jess told him to get his education. Danny would be his farmer. Eddie turned six in 1936 and, although he was so much smaller than the Knight boys, they treated him well and commented on how spunky he was. They did seem to like him and looked after him.

Chapter 11

๛

Riding the Rails

Orville was still in western Texas when Raymond's letter came to General Delivery. His appearance had changed a lot. Gone was the dark youthful figure; and now he was a slightly stooped, rail thin man who could have been fifty instead of just under forty. He read the news sent to him and sat with his head in his hands for most of that evening. He half expected bad news in these hard times, but finding out that little Leo, Bill, Art, and Ted were lost forever was just not something his mind could handle. He read the letter over and over. Raymond didn't say anything about Frances except to say she was okay and they had another son after he left. When not working, he thought of little else the next week and began planning to return home. He had over two hundred dollars, and the job could last another two to six months. He'd decide soon.

The winds and weather in the Texas panhandle shut down Orville's work for the rest of the winter in early 1937. With his nearly two hundred and fifty dollars carefully concealed on his body, he decided if he didn't go now he might never make it. He'd gotten somewhat accustomed to staying in one place for a while. He didn't look forward to starting the hobo's life again of hitching rides on freights, especially in these cold months. His experiences of the past had not all been favorable as he rode the rails. He'd shared his life with New York bankers, Georgia croppers, and people from all walks of life who had nothing else to do except find the next meal. He had lived in cardboard communities called Hoovervilles. People putting the blame for the collapse of the economy on the former President named them. Once in a while a kindly farmer had let him share the barn with the animals for a week or two at a time, but most of the time he was hunting for food and seeking shelter wherever he could find it.

Most hoboes were just survivors like himself, but there were also those so hopeless that it wasn't unusual to find a body along the tracks, either hanging on a tree or mutilated by train wheels. He'd talked with hundreds of men over the years and shared many a fire and can of beans. He considered himself a loner, though, and few of these acquaintances lasted more than a week. Beside the elements and the need for work and food, there were times when the railroad conductors and brakemen, on orders from their bosses, chased the non-paying customers out of the freight cars. Mostly this was done at a stop, but there were some who had been known to club the hobo and toss him off headfirst while the train was moving.

Orville heard stories around the fires that made him wonder about the humanity of man. He hadn't had any personal bad experiences, although he'd been chased from the rail cars on occasion. Once or twice he had to abandon his ride while the train was still moving in order to avoid detection. That's why he was reluctant to start, but knew he had to. The weather was decent the first few days as he zigzagged his way by riding the rails in one direction, walking a while, and then finding another track headed in the direction he needed to go. Progress was slow, but he wasn't about to spend his money on travel. It was bad enough that he had to use some of it to eat on, so he did it sparingly.

He knew he was somewhere in Kansas by the end of the first week, and he then headed east on a slow freight. The weather had gotten much colder, and he didn't have any traveling companions. They must be wintering in the Hoovervilles, trying to survive. He was in an empty car, but the door was broken and wouldn't close. He heard voices and footsteps approaching on the top of the next car. He just huddled quietly in the corner when a burley looking uniformed man swung in through the door. The man had apparently seen him jump on the freight at the last stop because he didn't hesitate in coming to this car. He pulled a club from his belt and in an ugly voice said, "You bums all need to be taught a lesson you won't forget. You're no good for anything. I'm going to do my part to see that you won't be stealing rides again soon." He approached Orville and swung the club at him, but it glanced off the side of the car and Orville only received a hard rap on a well-padded arm. Orville moved quickly and hit the man at the knees with his shoulder sending him sprawling backward. Orville jumped over him and went out the door without checking the speed of the train or what the rail bed looked like. He didn't have time. He landed on his bad leg first which gave way, and as he hit the pain went through his body like a knife. He might have hit a large rock, but he'd never know because he tumbled through the dead weeds for several yards before he stopped. Breathless and in severe pain, he could only lay there. After a while, the cold began seeping into his bones and he knew he'd have to move or freeze. He tried to get up but he couldn't, that only made the pain worse. He started crawling on one arm pulling the bad leg behind him back toward the rails. He really thought he had come to the end of the line this time.

Orville had pulled himself as far as he could when he saw lights and thought a train was coming. Instead, less than fifty yards from where he was, a car passed and the thought of a highway energized him enough that he could crawl that last fifty yards. It was a highway and more lights were approaching. He tried to think what he could do to get attention. In desperation he pulled off his heavy coat and with all his strength flung it in the air in the path of the oncoming vehicle, which turned out to be a slow moving truck. Under his breath, he uttered, "Please God", and saw the truck swerve to avoid the object. The truck did brake to a stop to check out what they had almost hit. What they heard was Orville calling to them for help. Two men lifted him into the truck as he sank into unconsciousness. He awoke in a hospital in southern Kansas, where he found out that the knee would have to be permanently fused and the leg was badly broken again. In a lot of pain, he agreed to have it done and when it was all over he was penniless again. For all his effort, hope had just run out. Unable to work and broke, he reluctantly sent a telegram to Raymond telling him of his problem. The message read, "Broke, unable to work, leg in a cast, can you help?" Raymond's response was, "I'm coming as soon as I can, don't disappear again."

Raymond's duties in March were less demanding, but he did need a break in the weather to travel safely to Kansas. He drove over to talk to Frances because he didn't want her to be surprised to hear about Orville being back into the area. He owed her that. She took the news solemnly, and asked what Raymond planned to do since Orville obviously couldn't provide for himself. Raymond said he was going to take care of him until he got better. He owed that much to his brother. "Raymond, I got my life in control now, and I don't want any trouble," she said. "My son doesn't know him, and there's no reason for him to try to be a father at this time. Have him stay away from us." Raymond said he'd make sure that Orville understood this. "If anything needs to be said, I'll be the go-between," he said. He made the trip the next week to bring Orville home.

Chapter 12

☙❧

The First Clue

Frances' brother Willis had been a teacher in a town south of Charleston for the last six years. After teacher's college, he'd bounced around from one little rural school to another until he found a position in the high school in Greenup. There he'd met a fellow teacher, and in six months they were married. They now had two small children of their own. Frances had only seen him twice in the last three years, but she was happy for him and proud that he'd made it as a teacher. She had thought he'd make a good one.

In the early fall of 1936 he and a couple of other teachers were sent to attend a teachers' conference in Terre Haute, Indiana on the campus of another teachers' college. It was a two-day conference, and part of the value was the interchange with different teachers from all over the area. He had dinner with two of them from the Terre Haute area. In their exchange he shared that he was from Charleston and that he'd attended Eastern at Charleston. One of his dinner companions, Jim Tabors, told him he had a student who talked about coming from Charleston, an Arthur Newman. Willis tensed when he heard this and carefully worded his questions about the boy and his age. Jim said he was in the 8ᵗʰ grade and supposed he was about twelve or thirteen. He was a slight boy with dark hair and shorter than most of his class mates, "Did Willis know him?" he asked. Willis just said, "I don't think so," but in his mind he felt that maybe he had stumbled on information that he wasn't really sure he wanted. What was he going to do about it? He was sure of one thing: the name Arthur Newman would be a name he would not soon forget. He was troubled as he went home and didn't share the story with his wife or anyone. He was afraid it would only stir things up, and he wasn't sure he wanted to do that. He was a praying man, and this would probably take a lot of that.

Most of the time Willis was too busy with his family and his teaching to consider Frances' situation, but at times he had a nagging guilt of what he knew and wasn't telling her. He felt in his heart that it would be wrong and had potential for a lot of problems if Frances were to know where Art was. Still, she was his sister; and he knew she lived in agony at times over her missing boys, their health and their welfare. Losing these boys had left a big hole in her life.

Now the news that Orville had come back had only compounded the problem. He didn't know what to expect from this guy who had disappeared for years and really had no right to anything as far as Willis was concerned. So far it had all been very quiet. Willis hoped it would stay that way because, after much thought, he was considering doing one thing. He wondered if he could secretly explore this information about Art by having a private detective spend a little time in Indiana. Would the information be helpful and possibly even a way of closing a wound for Frances, or would it just be a waste of money? If the detective found anything bad, it never needed to get beyond him. It was a tempting thought. After many months of praying and talking it over with his wife, he started the ball rolling. He hoped it was the right move.

Chapter 13

❧❧

The Watson Story

The streets in Webster Groves, Missouri, were all but impassable that March morning in 1937. Webster Groves was a wealthy suburb of St. Louis, and the Watson's had lived there in their large twelve-room house since the war. Mr. Watson had developed a patent that was critical to the war effort in 1917, and it had been financially beneficial. He was an engineer by education and training. Although he could have held out for multi-millions for his invention, his love of country had come first.

He was reasonably wealthy now from his own business, but wealth was never what was important to him. It was all about family and service to his country and community. He was fifty-five years old, and his wife Kathryn was four years younger. They had met in college, married after graduation, and settled in St. Louis where he worked for a bridge building company. He enjoyed the work but wasn't challenged, so at the age of thirty he set up shop in a small shed behind their rented house and started experimenting with new ideas. They had a son who was grown up now and had taken over the engineering firm he had founded in 1920. Charles, Mr. Watson's given name, was proud of his son, and had been content to enjoy life and watch him grow as a man and citizen. About ten years earlier, when their son Charles Junior had married and left the nest, his wife had become insistent that they were still young enough for more children. Of course, the doctors had said years ago that this wasn't likely. Kathryn wasn't to be denied, though, and pressed the possibilities of adoption. It was more of a discussion than a search between she and Charles for several months and other family members knew it was being considered. One day Kathryn's sister living in Charleston, Illinois, informed her about these four brothers who had been left at the children's home and had become eligible for adoption. Kathryn wouldn't rest until she knew more. Soon they were driving to Charleston, about a hundred and twenty miles away, before Charles realized the decision had been made. She was excited at the prospect, and her sister had said they were the nicest children with good manners and apparently all very bright. She was thinking that two boys would even be better, especially in the ages mentioned which were 5 to 10. Instead of the direct approach, Charles contacted a local attorney to act as a middleman and waited on him to search out the facts for them. It wasn't long before the attorney returned to the office to explain that two of the boys were already gone, but the facts stated by Kathryn's sister were correct. Only the nine-year-old and five-year-old remained. One was rather tall and dark, and the other small for his size. Both were highly recommended by the superintendent. After that report, Kathryn went into high gear, and a week later they returned home to Webster Groves with their son William. Her one compromise was that she settled for one instead of two. They had never regretted their action and considered it one of the luckiest moves of their lives. William was very special and very accepted by all the family. His mild manners and shy smile won them over quickly. That morning, as Mr. Watson gazed out at the drifts, he was wondering if he and William could shovel out the drive. It was too bad that the city didn't have better snow removal equipment. Maybe he could work on that.

Chapter 14

જ્જ

Leo Found a Home

Leo was not afraid of hard work. He'd always done it and, even though he was small, he always did his share. Despite the need to help his dad, he'd managed to get his education and this was the year he'd graduate from high school. He'd felt awkward and lost when the Swenson's had taken him home to northern Illinois. They both spoke with heavy Swedish accents, and at first he wasn't sure whether they wanted a son or an unpaid servant. They were so different from the people he'd grown up with. Kind words and smiles were few and far between. He arose every morning, milked twelve cows and did the feeding before going to school.

The Swenson's had come to this country as a young couple in 1911 and had paid for their trip by working for their sponsors for two years. What they learned was the dairy business. By hard work they eventually had bought their own thirty-five acres, and started with a bull and two heifers. They were small- time operators but they were frugal and didn't need much. Their hard work had paid off.

Unable to have their own children, they were reconciled to being childless, but in their upper thirties their lives changed dramatically. The couple that had sponsored them to come to America had stayed in touch over the years and showed up at their home in 1931. They had a young boy with them and told them the story of how they'd heard of a family in need and had stepped up to help. Although they were in their early sixties, because they had financial stability, were well known, and had a long history of humanitarian pursuits, they'd been allowed to take this young boy home with the intent to adopt. Almost immediately, Mrs. Gray had been diagnosed with terminal cancer. Rather than take the boy back, they came to the Swenson's knowing they were still childless. The boy would be much better off with them than living in an orphanage for the next seven or eight years, and they wanted to persuade the Swenson's to step in where they couldn't. The Swenson's held the Grays in high regard, but this was all too new for them. They wanted a day or two to think it over.

Alone they discussed the fact that they were ill equipped to be parents, especially of an eleven-year-old boy. They also realized that the Grays had come to them and they owed that couple so much. It was obviously very important to them. How could they refuse them? Besides, the boy was also of the age that he could be of some real help around the dairy. They weren't without compassion and couldn't ignore the fact that others had helped them along the way. In the end it was their loyalty to the Grays and the fact that they truly believed they could do better than an institution for a young boy. The Grays handled the legalities, and the couple that had reconciled themselves to a life without children, now had a son.

They didn't develop a warm, loving relationship, at first. After a rocky start, the young man who felt he'd been abandoned had to learn to adjust. Now mutual respect had grown and a true fondness existed. They had encouraged him to get his education, and now he was ready for graduation. What would come now was yet to be seen. Leo would be an adult and could decide what he wanted to do, although the Swenson's were in no hurry for him to leave them. Leo's only plans were to work and try to make a life better than what he had experienced to date. His dad had deserted him, his mother had given him away, and he had lost his brothers. Life had to be better that that.

After graduation Leo stayed around home and helped his dad for a couple of years, along with other work he could pick up on neighboring farms. It was a good life for him with low stress, but he began to want something else. He had always yearned for some excitement and adventure. At one point he had even contacted Mr. Kirkley at the

Charleston Children's Home to find out about his brothers. Mr. Kirkley was polite to him, but when it came to getting any information from him, he had hit a stone wall. He couldn't or wouldn't share anything with him about his brothers. Leo didn't ask about his mother.

Not succeeding there, he pursued the idea of getting away by joining the service. In early 1940, with his parent's approval, he joined the Navy. The country was having a small military build up, and he thought this would give him an opportunity to see the world. He wanted to avoid working in the dirt; he'd had a lifetime of that, so the sea was what he opted for. He received his basic training and was lucky enough to get posted to Hawaii. Rumor was that this was paradise and considered the best duty for a sailor. After a few months, he decided he liked the life and at the end of his term he thought he would probably re-enlist to make it a career. Toward this goal he applied himself and was given top ratings by his superiors. Although rank was slow in the peacetime Navy, eventually he knew that he would move up the ladder.

Chapter 15

❧❦

Before the War

It was 1938 and the work and living arrangement that Frances had with the Knights was comfortable, and much of their interaction felt like family. In time Big Jess became more like an older brother to her. Their conversations had become more like that with a certain amount of banter, and give and take. He had never been a warm and cozy person, but seemed happy to have a good and reliable housekeeper, and he was feeling this could be a permanent situation. In fact, when his oldest son Jim left home, he insisted that Eddie take his room. Big Jess had already added a new pantry to the kitchen, and the old one was converted to a closet and dressing room for Frances. In his own way he had encouraged Frances to have lady friends over as well as other family. She always made it a point to make sure she wasn't interfering with his schedule before she did so. She found she could even discuss her boys and the desire she'd have until she died to locate them again. He secretly thought she was asking for more heartbreak, but that was her business and he'd support her in any way he could.

He wondered what, if any, her husband's coming home would have on his household. Not knowing the man, he guessed they would cross that bridge when they came to it. She told him that she had informed his brother Raymond that she didn't want anything to do with Orville and to keep him away from her. Surprisingly the only message that

Raymond had brought after Orville had been home about four months was to ask her if she'd divorce him. Raymond said Orville didn't feel he deserved her and that he wouldn't contest anything she wanted to do. She never thought about divorce. After the initial surprise, she told Raymond that she needed to talk to her pastor about it and get some needed guidance before she would answer. She didn't feel the need to hurry.

People were going back to work, either what some called government make-work or work that was directly related to the war in Europe. New factories were starting up, and there was more activity than Frances had seen in years. Her life was much the same, but she had granted Orville a divorce based on desertion and didn't ask for anything.

Uncle Adren had scraped rock bottom in the late depression years and finally took up construction work to feed his family. He worked on some of the local highways the government was building, but it wasn't very regular. He still did some sharecropping, but with his eight kids to feed he needed to find other work. His oldest son Franklin spent two years in C.C. Camps (Conservation Corps) that Mr. Roosevelt had started. What he earned helped feed the family and keep them together. Through it all, though, he was still the same man. Weather-beaten and tough as rawhide, he was always there with a smile and word of encouragement for Frances when she needed a lift. Life was hard for his wife who was struggling to raise their eight children with the Christian values she wanted them to have. She was a good woman and good for Uncle Adren because she held him accountable.

Some family she never saw. Uncle Jesse, Adren's older brother, lived over in Windsor and for years had a political job with the state in Springfield. Frances wasn't sure what he did, but supposedly his good record in the world war was helpful in getting him hired. Her mother's other six siblings were spread all over a three-county area and nearby Indiana. She saw them periodically, and in 1918 the family had started a tradition of meeting at least once a year at an extended family reunion.

Frances had saved a little over the years while working for Big Jess. She had accumulated about a hundred and fifty dollars and secretly hoped that one day soon that would become a part of the finders' fees. That's what she called the funds she expected to spend to locate her sons. She had discussed this at length with her dad and knew that one day she would start the search that was so long in coming. Her dad had already been to the courts and lawyers for her. He wanted to see what could be done about finding the boys and had only met with resistance at every turn. In her commitment Frances knew that where there was a will, there would be a way. She had not survived this long by just lying down and not trying. One Sunday in August, she was attending a family dinner for Robert who was home for a visit from Colorado. Willis and Evangeline were also there with their families, and she received the biggest surprise without even paying one cent in finders' fees.

Chapter 16

৵৽

Pearl Harbor

On the morning of December 7, 1941, Leo was on a destroyer sitting at anchor in Pearl Harbor, Hawaii. For the first time in his life, he had developed close buddies and was enjoying life with frequent liberty into Honolulu and other locations around the islands. As he had anticipated, it was an adventure and he'd never been happier. He wrote home about once a week to his parents and shared all of this with them. As he had matured, he had learned to appreciate them more and more. They seemed to take pride in his accomplishments and looked forward to the letters he wrote.

This particular Sunday morning, he was awakened from a deep sleep in his rack (bunk bed) by sheer bedlam. There were thunderous noises all around, and he struggled to get his clothes on and get up on deck to see what was happening. He was colliding with sailors trying to do the same thing when the intercom and bells started sounding, advising everyone that this was not a drill and to take their battle stations. Half stunned and wondering what was happening, he made his way to his station.

Back in the states, William heard about Pearl Harbor as he was having lunch in his dormitory at seminary. As a second year student, he was doing well and was surer than ever that he had answered the right call. It had been at church camp, when he was sixteen, that he made his commitment to attend a Bible college. He told his parents on returning home that he wanted to be a minister of the gospel. They sat down and had a long serious conversation with him at that time, and again later to determine if his commitment remained firm. In the end they supported him in his obvious heartfelt decision, and when he graduated from high school they were there to help him get into the college of his choice.

He had always been taught service first by his parents, and, despite their wealth, that was the way they lived. The community of Webster Groves and even the greater St. Louis area had heard about and respected the Charles Watson family because of their involvement and support of humanitarian and other worthwhile causes. What happened on December 7 was to change William's life and everyone else's. But in his case, it was to interrupt his education for a greater cause.

At Christmas, after the semester ended, he went home to once again sit with his parents and explain what he felt called to do. They went with him to their church where they talked to the pastor and later to the elders. There was no hesitation by anyone who knew William to help him, and no one tried to change his mind. He truly felt it was his calling. His desire was to be ordained by his church so that he might serve the fighting men and women as a chaplain in the U.S. Army. In February, of 1942, he left for the army. Because he was an ordained minister, he was sent directly to officer's training school. By the first of August he was the youngest chaplain in the army. His first assignment was in a replacement depot in Maryland. He had made the right decision for all the right reasons. His maturity surprised even his parents who had never doubted his dedication.

Chapter 17

꩜

The War Years

Art couldn't wait to get into the military. All his friends were joining, and he had stayed home an extra year because of his parent's wishes. He'd been lucky enough to get a job in the larger of the two Terre Haute hospitals as an orderly. He didn't have any formal training but liked being around the medical people and listening in on their conversations while he was working.

The medical personnel began noticing the slight young man for his efforts and started calling him by his first name. They liked to tease him about being sweet on this little nurse or that young nurse's aide, and he took it all in fun. In fact, he was kind of sweet on Molly who worked second shift. She was a couple of years older than he, having completed nurses' training. She was cute, petite, and friendly. Beside her he even felt tall, which he wasn't. He was about five foot five with a fairly muscular build and a solid 135 pounds.

Art had been with the hospital about six months in 1942 when he got up the courage to ask Molly out. He was slightly surprised that she said yes. Because her only nights off were Sunday and Monday, their first date was a matinee on Saturday at the local theater. They didn't realize that the movie playing, "Gone With The Wind," was so long. That resulted in her being thirty minutes late to work that Saturday.

This really got them teased by the doctors and nurses, who questioned what they'd really been doing.

Their relationship was progressing slowly, which was unusual at a time when romances were escalated by the war. Because of the chance of the fellow leaving on the next troop train or ship, young couples got in a hurry. Art was very levelheaded for his age. Even though Molly had been to his home to meet his folks, he knew things in the world were much too chaotic to be making lifelong commitments and decisions. Molly seemed fine with all that. She at 23 had experienced romances, but found this guy pretty special and worth waiting for.

Art was the only one that wasn't unhappy when his number came up at the draft board in late 1942. In their last days together, he shared all he could with Molly of his life and his hopes for their future with the hope that she would wait for him. On a Sunday he and Molly were out together in his father's car when on a whim he started driving west on Route 40. He'd never been back to Charleston, but he wanted to share this place with Molly also.

It was almost a two-hour drive, and he was using his father's rationed gas to do it, but somehow he needed to share this with her. He managed to locate the town and the children's home without any problem. The town was bigger and busier than he remembered. As they drove the streets, he explained that somewhere in these houses were probably relatives of his mother and father. He remembered Mr. Kirkley's name and, at the last minute decided to go by and check him out. Boys were playing in the yard at the home, and a lady was in charge inside. When he asked if Mr. Kirkley was around, she explained he was gone for the afternoon but would return in time for supper if he wanted to wait. That wasn't possible and, having shared what he wanted to share they returned home. He didn't want to chance getting lost, so he passed up the notion of trying to locate the Canaan house. This trip had been special to Molly, and she thanked him for taking her to this place of his childhood. He told his parents of their trip, and they were fine with it-although his dad said he'd probably have to walk to work for a week to make up for the gas Art had burned. Art knew he didn't really mind though, because he had a very special relationship with his dad.

It wasn't long before Art was in basic training in Texas, a long way from home. With his hospital and medical experience, the Army did something it didn't often get credit for doing. They made a right decision and decided to train this young man as a corpsman, or medic as the GIs knew them by. Medics were in big demand; and by 1944, he had been in Africa, Sicily, and would soon land in Italy. He had been mostly in field hospitals and medical units behind the lines, but he was now assigned to a unit that would be among the first to go ashore at Anzio.

Art's story was the surprise that Frances got from Willis at the family reunion. Willis didn't give her any names or places but let her know that Art was alive and well, and very happy in a warm and secure family environment. He made it clear to her, that the reason he told her this was so she would get some comfort from it. Despite her wanting to know particulars, he wouldn't give her any more information. He promised that he would pass on any news that he could, of Art, in the future.

Over the years, Willis had maintained his contacts in Terre Haute who had initially researched Art's story for him. From time to time he would ask for, and receive, updates that he would use to assure Frances that all was well. He'd told her about Art joining the army and the fact that he was a medic, but he didn't elaborate on where he was. He didn't want his sister attempting to locate him. After all, she was still a mother and he didn't want her tempted beyond what she could handle.

With his busy life and teaching job in Charleston, Willis had not made any recent inquiries. He was stunned by a correspondence from his contact in Terre Haute, complete with newspaper clippings from the Terre Haute paper about a hometown man dying a hero's death in Italy. There in the clippings was the story of Art, who had died on the battlefield trying to save a soldier under fire. The story said he had already been given a silver star for courage above and beyond the call of duty. In previous action he had saved three men in the crossfire of enemy automatic fire. Art had crawled to their assistance on three different occasions with morphine and assistance. The article went on to say he left behind his parents, Mr. And Mrs. George Newman of the city, and a special friend Molly Jones. Willis was shaken. He shared this sad news with his wife and wondered when, if ever, he could share this story with Frances. He said a silent prayer for Art, his parents and Frances.

Back on the east coast of the United States, Theodore, or Ted as he preferred being called, had already been accepted at VMI (Virginia Military Institute) for the fall of 1942. With his military training in prep school the past four years, he was really hoping for something more. His father, now a bird Colonel, was in the South Pacific as an aide to General MacArthur. After the Japanese had forced MacArthur off the Philippines, leaving many of his aides behind, he had gone to Australia where the Colonel had joined him. Ted was young enough to think that he, too, could be a military leader. At times his immaturity scared his mother, who tried to harness some of his ambitions. She didn't want him out there taking chances. She already had a husband in harm's way and she intended to keep her son at home and safe. She wasn't about to sign papers for him to enter the regular Army, and her husband agreed with her.

That is why Ted entered VMI that fall rather than go on active duty. At VMI he could train to be an officer and a gentleman. In four years, on mother's plan, he could become a career soldier like his father if he wanted. He didn't like this turn of events but decided to make the most of it. He did enjoy VMI, its traditions, the young ladies, and the Virginia countryside. He had a full social life that year. In June he turned eighteen and, despite his parent's wishes and influences, he joined the Army to do his part.

Almost immediately the Army tagged him as officer material, but he was never sure what other influence came into play in that regard. He was a Wainright, and he was sure some of the people making the decisions were classmates or friends of his father at one time or another. He graduated high in his class at Officers' Candidate School, and by that winter he had been commissioned as a Second Lieutenant in the U.S. Army. Soon afterward he was on a ship to England, where in the rain and fog he would be trained and give training to hundreds of soldiers.

The men in his platoon referred to him as the "young shave tail" behind his back. But in the six months they had been training together, they learned to trust this young man and admire his leadership skills.

Due to their readiness, his platoon was singled out for special duties and became one of the first Special Forces in Europe. They excelled in cliff repelling and underwater demolition. The troops didn't know what they were training for, but they were pretty sure it wouldn't be as tough as the training that this young lieutenant was putting them through.

On one night maneuver a large boat struck a smaller boat containing a squad of Ted's men, capsizing it into the bay. Ted was credited with jumping into the water and saving two of his men who were injured and drowning under the weight of their battle gear. For this he received a citation from the general, and gained new respect from his platoon and others in the company. His men were tired of training. After several delays they were finally on a small ship, among hundreds of larger ships, headed toward the French coast. It was June 6, 1944. Ted had just turned nineteen.

William had experienced a lot of things in the almost three years he had served as a chaplain. Some were too terrible to speak of, and some were soul enriching. He had served the last two years in the war zones of Africa and Europe. At first it had been difficult having one-to-one relationships with young men entering harm's way, knowing many would not be returning. He had grown with his job, and now the resolve they took to their job, their spirit and their faith, made him proud to know such men. He wanted to be a part of these men's lives. In these stressful times they wanted to grow closer to God, and he was inspired by many of them.

William himself had been promoted to Major, which meant that he did not have to work as close to the front lines. Bombing and the strafing behind the line was always dangerous, but not like front line duty. Still, when at all possible William would get as close as he could to the GIs in the trenches and foxholes. Many times he shared the wet, cold, and dangerous conditions that the front line men endured. He was always up among them for Sunday services and, even if it were only a squad of men, he still wanted to be there for them.

It was at one such service on a cold and muddy morning somewhere in Italy, that William and some men were caught in a deadly crossfire from the Germans. The Germans had counter attacked, causing a rapid retreat of the allies. The squad of men that William was with did not get the word to retreat, and were cut-off from the rest of the company. They were pinned down and shelled by automatic weapons fire, and those not killed immediately were dying. William lay bleeding and dying in the mud when a corpsman crawled up to him, checked his wounds, and gave him morphine for his pain. In his dazed and pain-wracked condition, the thought crossed his mind that he knew this medic. He then passed out as the morphine took effect. When he awoke he was in the Battalion aid station, breathing through his neck and with multiple injuries.

Only later when he was in the rear echelon recovering from his wounds did he hear the full story. The medic had saved his life by inserting a hollow tube in his trachea so he could breathe, then, unaided and under heavy fire, carried him to safety. The medic had kept him and two other soldiers alive until the allies' counterattack drove the Germans back. He got this story from one of the men saved with him, and William avowed that he would one day find that young man.

Two months later he visited the headquarters company to trace the corpsman and was able to determine his name: Arthur Newman of Terre Haute, Indiana. He also learned that he had been awarded the Silver Star with Clusters posthumously for later heroism under fire. He saw the man's military record and, noting the date and place of birth, realized that he was looking at his brother's army record. He was devastated to find out that the man who saved his life was his brother, who had lost his own life saving others.

William mourned his brother's death and prayed for his soul. He vowed then, that one day he would get to know the Newman family and tell them firsthand what their son had done for so many lives and families. He wanted to know this couple that had adopted this homeless boy and had done such a wonderful job of raising him to be the man that he had been. He wanted them to know how many parents owed him for their son's lives, and that included William and his family. He wanted to console Art's parents for their tremendous loss and do anything is his power to thank them. He paused in his thoughts and considered doing one more thing. When he got home, he'd contact somebody to see if his Grandmother McGrew were still living. He really wanted someone from Art's birth family to know about this young man and the tremendous bravery he had shown, even if that did expose his own life and story to people who might want to take advantage of him for some reason. He'd take the chance of some heartache because this brother was that important to him. For now, though, there were still men to reach and battles to be followed. He was coming off recovery and would soon be transferred to the front in France.

Chapter 18

❧❦

The War Ends

Ted was already at the front. On June 6 his company was among the first to hit the beaches at Normandy, albeit part of them were under the waterline attempting to disarm and remove as many mines as possible for the troops coming in. From there they assaulted the high slopes, attempting to make inroads from the beach. They scaled the cliffs to knock out the heavy artillery firing down on the thousands of troops on the sand. Many a good soldier and man lost their life that day on the sand. Ted's platoon had performed very well, but at the end of the day they had a 25% casualty rate. By the grace of God, Ted wasn't hurt. He wasn't a church-going man, although he did believe in God. At the end of this day, he did pause and thank God for the deliverance of himself and most of his men. He had seen many heroic deeds that day and also a few cowardly deeds, but he would always remember the former and forget the latter. His men had all performed above and beyond.

The next few days they pushed inland. When his battalion hit a snag or special circumstances, it was the platoon under Ted's command that was called on to meet the task of breaking the deadlock or eliminating the obstacle. By the first of October, optimism was high, and the guys were already talking about Christmas in Germany and home for Easter. Even Ted's letters to his father in the South Pacific were hopeful. His dad was quick to answer and caution him to not get overconfident with the German Army. They had been underestimated before.

Ted's unit was given the job to secure and hold a critical bridge so that the allied forces could advance with heavy equipment. They had to infiltrate behind enemy lines to do so and had successfully secured it when the German's did a massive offensive, called the Battle of the Bulge, in another sector. This was a major blow to the allies, and talk of home by Easter was quickly forgotten as many of Ted's friends lost their lives. After that experience, the march on Germany began in earnest and talk of home was put on the back burner. Though many of the bridges had been blown up by the enemy, the one Ted's unit had secured was not and was instrumental in the allies march.

If Ted had been attending Sunday services with his troops in the spring of 1945, he may have run into his brother William. Although he had only been six when he last saw his big brother, it was possible that he might have recognized him. The allies met up with the Russians in April 1945, and soon the victory in Europe was secured, leaving Ted wondering what his next assignment would be. He was hoping that he'd join the war in the Pacific where his father was. His father opposed the idea, but that was where the war was now and he was a military man. Soon after Normandy, Ted had been promoted to First Lieutenant and that was quite an accomplishment. He was not yet twenty-one.

At Pearl Harbor Leo had lost his ship when a single torpedo was dropped from a Japanese airplane and struck it in the middle. All but six of the sailors aboard had been saved, but Leo lost his best buddy that day. Most of the injuries were fire related as they abandoned ship into the burning inferno of the oil-covered bay. Leo was a good swimmer but had managed to swallow enough contaminated water to make him sick for a week. The hospital was needed for the badly injured, so he managed to rough it out and recover on his own. With so many ships sunk and so many sailors displaced, it took a couple of weeks to get organized and for the Navy to reassign all of the personnel. In the interim they had all pitched in and worked salvage, clearing debris wherever they could. Because Leo had gunnery training, he was assigned to a Battleship, the biggest ship afloat except for the aircraft carriers. Thankfully the carriers had been at sea on December 7, or they would have been easy targets for the bombs and torpedoes with all their aircraft on board. Leo's experience now became more important as replacements began arriving in the Pacific. He was quickly promoted and given greater responsibilities than ever before. By the end of the war, he was a Chief Petty Officer, but not before he had two other ships shelled and bombed from under him. He was involved in many major battles and island landings. He was there when General MacArthur retook the Philippine Islands. When the bombs were dropped on Hiroshima and Nagasaki, he was on shore duty back in Honolulu, his first reprieve in two years. He would long remember the celebration that took place there when the unconditional surrender was signed on the USS Missouri. Leo had not seen home in more than five years. When the first orders were cut to start sending the soldiers and sailors home, he was near the top of the list.

Chapter 19

❧❦

The Home Front

The gas rationing, the scrap drives, the war bond sales, and the victory gardens were all part of the war effort and way of life in the early forties in Coles County. Getting new tires for a car was all but impossible. Living without a radio or daily newspaper severely restricted the knowledge people in the rural areas had about what was going on in the world. Unless they had loved ones involved, people generally got their updates by word of mouth at the Sunday services or down at the town square. Many families had received letters from the War Department that either said their loved ones had been killed or wounded in action in some remote area of the world that they were not even familiar with. Death was final; but some of the badly wounded from the war would spend years in hospitals and rehabilitation centers, and many would never be the same again. Many homes were affected.

Frances did all she could to follow the war news. Big Jess's boys were directly involved, and she was sure somewhere her boys were in it also. She didn't know very many young men who had not been drafted and all of her boys, except Eddie, would have been draft age. She prayed often and fervently for them and others. Uncle Adren's son-in-law, his daughter Katherine's husband Louie, had been killed in Italy. His oldest son Franklin was in the South Pacific. Other family members were also fighting in Europe. Many homes hung banners in their windows showing gold stars for husbands and children who died in the war effort, and these homes became places of honor. Mothers who had lost children became known as Gold Star Mothers. Death touched many homes in the county but not the home she made with Big Jess, Danny, and Eddie. Had the war gone on another six months, it was likely that Danny would have been drafted. The bombing of Japan ended the carnage that had created so much grief.

By September 1945, the war was officially over. When William got back to the states from Europe, his first stop was Terre Haute, Indiana, even before he went on home to Missouri. He called Mr. Newman, explaining that his son Art had saved his life in Italy. William explained he was aware Art had lost his own life, and asked if he could come by and pay his respect.

They were gracious hosts and William could tell by talking to them that they had been great parents for Art. Early on in his visit, he also revealed the other reason he came and they were surprised and happy that they were meeting Art's brother. William filled them in on the background and stories of the Trapp boys of Coles County, and the reasons they were put up for adoption. In turn they told him about Art the teenager and man whom William had never known. They also told him about his girl friend Molly and their plans and aspirations. William couldn't tell them where the other brothers were because he didn't know, but he did tell them the full story of how Art had indeed saved his life and his subsequent search for Art. William was so thankful that he had made this trip and, with tears all around, he vowed to be back again for another visit. He invited them to look in on him anytime they could. He'd promised to keep them posted on where he was.

He then went on home to Webster Groves where the family gave him a hero's welcome, which he didn't feel he deserved. The only visible mark of his injuries that he had was a small u shaped scar on his throat where his brother had inserted a tube that saved his life. He would always remember that each time he faced a mirror. The family was very interested in all the details of his visit with Art's family and hoped that they, too, would have the opportunity to meet and visit with the Newmans. Although he had written all the details of his connection with Art in Italy, this man, who was also his brother, fascinated the family.

This led to their questioning him about his memory of his own youth. They had not done so before because they weren't sure he wanted to talk about it. But now they could see he still had real attachments to the memories and brothers of his childhood. He told them he was considering making some contacts in Coles County. He wanted Art's family there to know and appreciate the man Art Trapp turned out to be. He also wanted to honor Art's parents by telling as many as he could of them, and the wonderful son they had raised. William's family was very supportive and asked what they could do to help.

His mother came up with the idea of contacting her sister. William's Aunt Marilyn, who had told his parents many years ago about the children that were up for adoption, would probably know something. William's Aunt Marilyn had since moved to Champaign. When they called, she said that there were still people she stayed in touch with in Charleston and that she might be able to find a name or telephone number. In a couple of days she called back with the news that his grandparents were still alive and living in Charleston, as was their son Willis McGrew. The elder McGrew's were not well, but the son was a teacher in the local school system and she gave her sister a phone number for him.

Willis was still feeling the burden of Art's death, which he had not shared with Frances yet. It was nearing Christmas when he had finally decided what he had to do. One evening he was sitting at home when he received a long distance call and was asked if he was Willis McGrew, son of the Reverend and Mrs. William McGrew. Willis acknowledged that he was, and the caller went on to explain who he was. Willis sat in shock when the man said, "Uncle Willis, this is Frances' son William. Do you remember me?" He recovered quickly and joyfully said he did and that it was so good to hear from him. He had been thinking a lot about him over the years. Willis began to question him when William said, "There's too much to handle this way, but if it's convenient I'd like to drive over Saturday from St. Louis and visit with you." He did ask if his grandparents were available for a visit, as he'd like to meet with them also. Willis said, "Do you want your mother present also?" This time the silence was on the other end. William had thought his mother was dead all these years. When he finally ask about that, Willis apologized and said he'd forgotten the circumstances at the time. Willis assured him that she had indeed survived and would very much want to see him. William knew now there was more involved than what he had anticipated, but said he'd see them all on Saturday. Willis sat in silence after he hung up, wondering how he was going to break this news to Frances. He didn't sleep much that night.

The next morning he took off work and was slowly driving toward Oakland, still trying to formulate how he was going to tell Frances the news. As he drove back up the lane, things were quiet and there weren't any autos in the drive or garage. He assumed that Frances would be alone, which was good. Frances was surprised to see Willis getting out of the car on a weekday and concluded correctly that this was more than just a visit. Was something wrong with her parents? She opened the door before he knocked and hurried him in out of the cold. She gave him a hug, all the while studying his face. He looked deeply concerned. "Is it mom or dad?" she asked. He shook his head no and told her to sit down, because he had much to tell her.

He began slowly by telling about the discovery of the whereabouts of Arthur and what he had done over the years to keep track of him. He did this so he could reassure Frances about Art's welfare. He continued by telling he'd withheld some information from her in an effort to protect her from the anxiety he knew she would have. Frances felt a cold chill go down her neck as she listened to Willis and his explanations. The reason he was telling her all this now couldn't be good, and her dread built as Willis continued. "Art had been a medic in the army in Europe," He quietly said. "I've learned that Arthur died a hero's death in Italy over a year ago. When the time is right, I'll share the details with you." Frances slumped with her face in her hands. Willis moved beside her and placed his arm around her sagging and shaking shoulders. This went on for a long period of time and Willis remained silent and let her grieve. When her sobs had subsided, he began again by saying he had more news and felt her stiffen again. "This isn't bad news, though," and he told her about last nights call from William. "He wants to come to Charleston Saturday to meet with the family." This news, on top of the grief she was feeling was just so unreal that she could hardly process it all. She asked Willis to repeat what he just said, and he did. She started asking questions about William, one after another, but Willis could only hold up his hand and say, "I know nothing that I can tell you. Maybe Saturday we'll all get the answers."

He sat holding Frances for a while longer and then rose as if to leave. Frances knew he was struggling, so she made the next move. "Willis, you need to go now. I know you left school to come here, and I do need time to try and sort this out. Thank you for coming. I know it wasn't easy, and I'll see you Saturday. Your place, right?" Driving home, Willis wasn't satisfied with the way he had handled it. But at least now it was done. There just wasn't any good way to break that kind of news to any parent.

William started early from his home in Webster Groves and drove slowly. He wanted to give himself plenty of time to think. After making that call to his Uncle Willis and finding out that his mother was also still living, he had a couple of nights where sleep didn't come easy in anticipation of this visit.

He pulled into the driveway of the modest one-story home, driving his father's expensive pre-war auto that was still in excellent condition. Two vehicles were already there and William braced himself for what he knew would be an emotional meeting. The weather was cool, but it wasn't really the reason for the almost uncontrollably trembling he felt as he approached the door.

Meeting him at the door was a gentleman, rather portly, he could vaguely remember as his Uncle Willis. Standing just behind him was, without a doubt, his mother. Aged, heavier and her hair almost totally gray, she stood there. Without hesitation he went to her and hugged her long and hard. William could feel both their hearts pounding within their chest. She didn't speak, but the tears flowed down a face that had perhaps the warmest smile he had ever seen. Finally, she held him at arms length and examined every detail of this handsome son that she had thought lost to her for a lifetime. She couldn't believe what she was seeing and holding. For that moment at least, the ache in her heart for her lost son Art was soothed.

At the same time William was having difficulty holding his emotions in check. This was his mother who had loved him and nurtured him for over ten years of his life, and who had instilled in him much of what he was today. She was the influence that made him a minister of the gospel as much as any person alive. Their years apart now melted between them. Once again he was her son. At her elbow was his grandmother and he gently hugged her. Next to her was the man he concluded was his grandfather. He reached out and shook his hand. He was introduced to Willis's wife and family, and then was led directly to the dining room. They had a lot of sorting out and catching up to do, but grandmother insisted the meal comes first. His grandfather said grace. Willis raised the question over dinner about what line of work William was in. They were all amazed when he told him he was an ordained minister, and had been a chaplain in the army for four years. William could see his grandfather out of the corner of his eye sobbing with his head bowed. He reached over and took his hand. That gesture meant so much to the old man. Frances folded her hands as William was talking. She appeared to be praying and more tears were rolling down her face. In a real way, this revelation made her feel her life had just been justified.

It was a while before William broached the subject he had come to talk about. He timidly tried to bring up the topic of Arthur more than once. When Willis recognized what he was trying to do, he spoke up. "We know about Art, William, but we didn't know you did." They began to share their knowledge and William relayed his story of Art to them. He told in detail the full account of Art saving his life and his ensuing search for him. He had to stop more than once to regain his composure, and all listening were quietly weeping too. He told them of his visit to the Newman's in Terre Haute, and what he knew of these wonderful people. Frances wept openly, not being able to contain her grief any longer, but still concentrating on every word from William's mouth.

Later in the day William had some quiet time with her. He told her about his life and how he now understood the circumstances surrounding the adoption, which he didn't know as a child. They exchanged memories of his youth, and the time together flew by too quickly. Only much later did he ask about his father Orville. Frances told him of the developments in her life. She told him how she concluded, after much prayer and consulting with her pastor, to give Orville the divorce he sought. They had been divorced many years. He had remarried but she never did.

William thought to himself that he did not need to renew a relationship with this man, but he also would not harbor any resentment against his biological father. He assured his mother that, although he had wonderful parents whom he loved dearly, there was and always would be a place for her in his life and heart. He had thought that she was lost to him, and he didn't want that to happen again as long as God gave them breath. In fact, he told her that one day he would take her to Missouri to meet his parents. He wanted them to know her. It was late in the evening when he said his goodbyes and headed home, feeling very good about this reunion with his family members. He couldn't wait to share the experience with his folks.

Chapter 20

֍

The Remaining Two

When the ship anchored at San Diego, the sailors received a hero's welcome. Leo couldn't help but cry as he stood looking at the wharf. It had been five years ago that he had set sail from here and so much had happened since. He and some buddies disembarked, and for the next three days they were boys again, foolish and carefree. He would remember very little of what happened there; but when he woke up three days later, he knew it was time to call home. After the initial greeting and the joy of hearing their voices, he explained that while he was in California he wanted to spend a little time there. He might never make it back that way again. He was in the land of fantasy, and that was what he had seen of America these past years through the USO Shows and the Hollywood movies that made it to the South Pacific. He wanted a little time to himself, and this was the place where he could be uncommitted for just a while longer, and think about what he wanted to do with the rest of his life.

He checked into a hotel for a week, and spent the days exploring the countryside and the nights, the party side. This country and these people were certainly a lot different than those in rural Illinois, and he even debated putting down roots and staying even longer. At age twenty-six his attachments, other than his parents, were few and far between. Although he did sometimes think of his younger brothers, lost to him so long ago, he knew he couldn't dwell on the past. A big chunk of his life had been spent on the rolling waves of the South Pacific, and now he had to decide what to do with the rest. If on his way home he had a chance to travel to Charleston, he just might take it, but for now he'd enjoy where he was. Maybe he'd become a star, he chuckled to himself.

Leo had his fun, and then decided he wanted to go home. He was to change trains in St. Louis and had the opportunity to walk around the terminal awhile. The train schedule posted on the wall in St. Louis showed he could go north to Springfield, Chicago, and all points north, or he could catch one going east that would pass just south of Charleston. He had a strong urge to take that one, but at the last minute got on the northbound one. That was what his ticket was for and he'd have to change it if he went east. It was near Christmas and he'd already delayed getting home long enough. His family had been fine with his exploring the west, but he owed it to them to get there for the holidays. Unknown to him, as he was boarding the northbound, his brother William was within blocks of the station, headed east for his meeting with their mother. The brother, who was next to him in age, and whom he remembered best, was also thinking of Leo as he drove along. Would their paths ever cross again?

Thousands of miles a way, a younger man was also thinking of home. After the surrender in Europe, Ted knew he wouldn't be going home right away because tens of thousands of men had been there much longer than he and deserved to go first. He didn't want preferential treatment, and he didn't get it because he was assigned to police duty in a German city called Nuremberg. It was a lot different than anything he had done since joining the Army, but it had its challenges. This city would soon be on the world map. This was where the war crimes were to be investigated and the trials would follow. He saw some of the charged criminals almost daily on his job.

He had learned in letters from home that his father, who was now a general, had decided to take retirement and spend some quality time with his wife after an absence of several years. There were no shortage of opportunities for him as a general officer, but he opted for one that would give Ted's mother and him the best chance to grow old together. That opportunity came as a surprise to Ted. His father became the

Commandant of VMI, his old school. The Virginia Military Institute would give his father the stature and acclaim that he so deserved, and would be a wonderful social setting for his mother who loved pomp and circumstance. It was a perfect setting for both of them, and Ted could not have been happier. Even thinking selfishly, he still had connections there and perhaps some of those little Virginia belles would still be around when he got the chance to visit them.

By the time his rotation back to the states came in the spring of 1946, Ted had decided without a doubt what he wanted to do. He was just twenty-one and had his heart set on attending West Point. He'd already written his dad, and the applications were already pending with notable references from three generals of the army, including Eisenhower and MacArthur. Ted knew that nothing was certain in life, but there wasn't anyone betting against his chances of getting in with the class of 1950 beginning the fall of 1946.

After a few months of relaxation with his family, he was looking forward to a new challenge in his life, the Point. He had grown up a lot the last two years and, while he still enjoyed a good time, he had his priorities in line to do what needed to be done.

Chapter 21

❧⚘

West Point

Ted felt a little out of place with the rest of the plebes that September as the fall semester began at the Point. When he arrived after his summer at home at VMI with his family, he was looking forward to making new friends. He had lost track of many of his old ones, and some didn't return from the war. He met new people at some of the socials and parties his mother insisted on, some on his behalf and other more general occasions, but only one stood out now at the end of the summer. She was the teenage daughter of one of the VMI professors. He met her early in the summer and got to know her despite the differences in their ages. She was vivacious and pretty, and had a Southern charm that he thought witty and cute. They never dated as such, but they spent a lot of time in each other's company on campus. She was only seventeen, but he vowed to himself that he could wait for this one. In four years when he graduated from the Point, she would be twenty-one. She was the one regret he had about leaving Virginia, but he also faced a bright future and challenges that he couldn't wait to get started with. There would be little time for girls and romancing that first year because he was determined to be the best at this career he had chosen.

To his knowledge, Ted was one of only six veterans entering West Point that fall of 1946. Most were entering directly out of high schools and prep academies and in many cases were barely eighteen years old.

One of the vets was his roommate, the son of a congressman from Ohio who didn't need his father's influence to get accepted, as Ted was soon to find out. He had not been in a war zone due to his father's pulling some strings. He wasn't very happy about that, but his abilities were soon to make him noticeable as a plebe and a competitor that Ted would have to cope with. His name was Joe Brown, and he told Ted he would have preferred combat to the paper-shuffling job he'd had stateside. It would have meant a lot to Joe to have something comparable to Ted's army record. He was a physical specimen along with being a real brain, but he respected his roommate and thought him a worthy competitor. The feeling was mutual. Joe decided against playing football in order to excel academically, and he became the best possible role model that Ted could have asked for in study habits and dedication to the corps.

College was college when it came to hazing incoming freshmen. Ted had already experienced that at VMI and now was prepared for it again. It was subtle at first, but both he and Joe noticed that they seemed to draw a bye (got preferential treatment) on some of the nonsense handed out by the upper classmen, probably in deference to their veteran status. They didn't mind. In fact, they were encouraged over coffee and at different times to share their experiences with the upper classmen. They didn't ask for favors and didn't expect them, and their classmates never showed any form of resentment toward them. At the end of that first year, they were both among the top of the class in performance in every category, but he was always one step behind Joe.

In the spring of 1947, the Academy had an invitation for two cadets to attend a White House function honoring two new recipients of the Congressional Medal of Honor. This was an invitation normally reserved for the senior cadets nearing graduation. But because the Academy had two outstanding veterans of the war, the decision was made to send them. Ted and Joe were selected to go. Also attending would be other Congressional Medal winners who had previously been decorated.

In full cadet dress uniform they were driven to the White House in a staff car. They were shown into the Yellow Room that was traditionally used for banquets of this nature. He and Joe separated, as was protocol so as to better represent the Point. Ted found himself sitting next to a young man not much older than he who was about the same size. He introduced himself to the man wearing a nametag with the name of Audie Murphy on it. Ted knew him to be the most decorated soldier of WWII. He'd heard the name and had seen the pictures in the Stars and Stripes newspaper distributed to the soldiers in Europe and even in newsreels. He felt honored to have the privilege of sitting next to him and told him so. As they talked, Ted was struck by the quiet humility the man exuded. Before long, he sensed a bond with the man having dinner across the table from him. In their short lifetime, they had been to a war and had experienced many of the same things.

Audie told him that after receiving his battlefield commission to Lieutenant, he was at various times questioned by his superiors about his interest in a military career. This led to a discussion of the possibility of his attending the Academy, which he felt wasn't practical because of his lack of a quality education. Several general officers persisted, though, and before long he was buying into the idea and opinion that maybe he could go to the Academy. These dreams all vanished, however, on a hillside in Europe when he was wounded in the thigh and hip by enemy machine gun fire. The injury would keep him out of West Point, and he fully understood this was one deficiency that could not be overcome with tutors and time.

During the evening Ted asked Audie if he had ever visited the Academy, and he replied that the opportunity had never arisen. Ted said, "I think the doors would be open wide if you would like to visit." Audie replied, "That would be great." Ted excused himself for a few minutes and made his way across the room to a table where a highly decorated general was sitting. Audie turned his attention elsewhere, but then saw Ted approaching him with this same officer. He was introduced to the man, and this was when the young war hero received his personal invitation from the Commandant of West Point. As he shook Audie's hand, the general said, "Thank you, Mr. Murphy, from a grateful nation." He could only reply, "Thank you."

It was decided that he should come the following week, the week before Memorial Day, when the cadets were all still on campus. The general wanted to give him the full hero's treatment. Audie said he'd be pleased to come, but asked him to play down the hero thing. "I was just a scared boy who loves his country, trying to protect his men." Ted and Audie cemented a lifelong friendship that night, and would exchange correspondence with occasional visits when Audie was on the east coast.

Ted learned that Audie's life was changing rapidly. He was collaborating with a writer on his life story, and Hollywood was already interested in making the film. This young man had the looks, the quiet charm, and the national acclaim to sell tickets at the box office. Ted thought this was only right after the sacrifices he had already made for his country. He'd have to leave his Texas roots behind, but this was a man whom the whole world would soon know.

The second year at the Academy was like the first for Ted, except there were more responsibilities, harder studies, and fewer classmates. Many had not made it to year two. Joe was there, and once again they were roommates and competing, but also helping each other. They had become very close friends. They had an interesting summer with mandatory summer camps, but Ted also had time with his parents.

His long distance friendship with Audie was still going strong. His little Virginia belle had now graduated from high school, and Ted's interest in her had not waned. They dated a few times that summer. He hoped she could make it to the Point for some of their socials that year, but for now she had chosen the college in Richmond at the southern end of the state. He told Joe all about her and how she was even more beautiful than ever. If Ted had his way, they would be engaged before the year was over.

Joe had no problem finding women friends. There wasn't much he lacked-except in Ted's opinion-a little sincerity and compassion. It wasn't noticeable until you got real close to him, as roommates are apt to do. Of course, no ones perfect, and Ted felt lucky to have such a friend. At midyear Joe was promoted to the top of the class, and Ted had no doubt that this man would one day be the General of the Army. His coat tails would be good ones to hang onto.

His Virginia belle was named Donna. Despite his urging she didn't make it up to a social until the spring, although he had seen her over the holidays. She was in big demand in Richmond with sorority life and many beaus. Ted cautioned her, with tongue in cheek, about dating too much and not making grades. She didn't want to flunk out. He was kidding, of course, but he was also a little jealous. Donna could give as well as take, though, and on more than one occasion had told him to buzz off and go polish his old cannons. In the spring she did come up, and they doubled with Joe and his date to the spring social and had a good time. She and Joe hit it off well, too, perhaps too well.

At first Ted didn't notice, but it became a habit for Joe to see him writing Donna and telling him to say hi from Joe. At other times he had other comments for her. Finally Ted told him if he had so much to say, maybe he'd better write his own letter. They laughed it off, and one last time to prod Ted, Joe said, "Just tell her I miss her beautiful blue eyes."

Ted heard from Audie and learned he was attending acting school and had signed a big contract with a movie studio to make a picture a year in Hollywood. His own book and movie were being held off until a future date. Meantime, they wanted him for westerns and other small parts. The release of the book would be timed to help sell the movie when it was ready. He had come to visit Ted at VMI the previous summer, and had the young ladies chasing him and the cadets trying to imitate him. Ted's own father had been very impressed with the young man and hoped that the Hollywood scene would not ruin him as it had so many others.

Audie was interested in Ted's story. From time to time he tried to draw it out of Ted. He said that his experiences in writing his autobiography had awakened his creative juices, and he wasn't content just to write about himself. He knew enough about Ted to think he had a story, too. He also wanted to write mysteries and historical novels, and didn't know where all of this might lead. Once he got started, he didn't want to stop. He pumped Ted more about his life, and Ted had to stop to think of what he remembered about his early life. It wasn't much. Audie encouraged him to commit in writing what he could remember, and then tell of his parents and the war years. It might make a good story, and he chidingly told Ted that he just might make a movie about Ted's life. Ted didn't think that was likely.

Chapter 22

☙❧

Time to Move On

In the summer of 1947, Danny came home with the news that Orville had remarried. He had heard it in town. That news didn't bother Frances. Later, when she learned that he had repurchased their little farm back from the bank and had built onto the house, there was some resentment. She had lost her youth in that house. She asked forgiveness for these feelings, but this man had never shown the slightest interest in getting to know Eddie or finding her sons. She couldn't understand that. He had not caused her any problems since his return and she was thankful for that.

Danny was the farmer his dad had hoped for, but the changing times had made a difference for the small farmer. A 160-acre farm was a lot to farm with horse-drawn plows and planters. At that time it supported the family very well. Now with modernization, more acreage was needed just to pay for the equipment. The small farmer was up against competition from corporate farming. Danny had taken a job in the Charleston shoe factory and had worked up to foreman. He had worked there since high school in addition to helping his dad. He knew that the farm was not going to support two families. One Sunday he had come home with a girl. It wasn't long before Danny was married and starting a family of his own. He moved to a home he purchased nearer his job in Charleston, leaving Big Jess alone with Frances and Eddie.

One cold evening as they sat around the stove, Frances asked the question that had crossed her mind over the years. "Jess, why didn't you ever remarry?" He looked at her and shrugged. "I guess I just never found anyone like my wife who could replace her. She was special. I never considered myself the marrying kind before she came along and changed my mind. Never had that feeling with anyone else," he said.

Frances then told him what was really on her mind. She knew he didn't need a full-time housekeeper anymore with the boys all gone. She was thinking about moving in with her folks to help care for them. Her dad was bedridden, and her mother was not really well enough to take care of him properly. Also, Eddie would soon be out of high school and most likely would move on. He had said he wanted to go out west. What little housekeeping Big Jess really needed she could come out once a week and do. Cooking for one was easy, and she knew he could handle that. She could help out on cleaning days by preparing food ahead for him. He wouldn't starve. Big Jess just listened and said when she was through, "Frances, we go back a long way, but you should do what you need to do." The next day over breakfast he added that he knew the situation with her folks and thought that taking care of them was the right thing to do for now. She started making plans to move. It was decided that with just a few months of school remaining, that Eddie could live with Big Jess and keep him company while finishing up.

Unexpectedly, Frances' father died before she had gotten moved. She still moved because her mother needed her now more than before. They needed to help each other through this mourning period. Her momma and dad had been a dedicated couple for many years. Frances was surprised in a way at the number of friends who called on them to express their gratitude for so many things that the Reverend had helped them through. That was a comfort to her. In recent years, Frances and her father had grown close.

Her folks had always lived on a shoestring, and the hard work that her mother had to do had severely weakened the woman that had not been well for years. Her dad never did have another full-time church. But when the miracle of healing had occurred between she and her dad, forgiveness had also come from many of the former friends and church members that had previously condemned him. He was asked to fill different pulpits from time to time on a temporary basis. This helped pay the bills when he couldn't get other work. His last illness put them in severe financial distress. To help out, Frances managed to get work at the shoe factory with Danny's help. She'd never worked outside the home. She soon learned that her employers did appreciate the hard work that she did. The money she made, plus a little subsidy from Willis, allowed her and her mother to pay off a small debt and meet current expenses.

It meant a lot to Frances to be able to contribute and care for her mother. For once she wasn't on the receiving end of someone else's goodness and charity, and she knew what Mrs. Snider must have felt like in helping her. It was rewarding in and of itself. She had often thought of that sweet woman that God had sent to her when she needed someone the most, so many years ago. As long as she had health, she knew that this was what she would do. Danny's wife took over the weekly cleaning for Big Jess, which worked out fine as Danny went out there frequently anyway. Things had worked out well. When Eddie graduated from high school that year, her direct ties to Big Jess was ended. She let him know how much she appreciated what he had done for her and her son. She would never forget this man who had done so much more for her than she could ever repay. His children would always have a special place in her heart also.

Despite his mother's objection, Eddie was set on going west with a classmate to explore the world. They planned to work their way toward Colorado by going during wheat harvest time. Frances could tell there was no changing his mind, so she encouraged him to look up his Uncle Robert, to write often, and to attend church regularly. The letters weren't all that frequent but she did hear from him at least once a month. The latest was from a place called Cheyenne Wells, Colorado. Maybe he was getting close to where Robert was.

Frances got a letter from the Newman's in 1948, telling her that they had exercised an option available to them to have Art's remains shipped home from Italy. If Frances wanted, they'd like for her to be part of the memorial service in Terre Haute. This would be a most fitting time, as they honored a son they both loved, to get acquainted. Frances, her mother, and Willis all planned to attend, as did William.

Although his church had ordained William, he had the opportunity-and now the GI Bill (which he didn't really need) to reenter seminary and get a degree in theology. He had much to learn from the Greek and Hebrew and wanted to be the most knowledgeable he could be. For this he moved to Cincinnati where he spent the next six years studying and getting an advanced degree. He was twenty-six years old when he started, but this was what was going to make him the happiest. The one drawback was leaving his parents, who were now getting up in years, but his schedule and financial resources allowed him to go home often. There was hardly a month that passed when he didn't travel through Terre Haute and Charleston on his way to and from Webster Groves.

He dated some, but nothing serious. He always attracted quality people and had many friends to socialize with. His main focus, other than family, was his education. He had committed his life to God, and his goal was to be the best prepared that he could be. His upbringing, his battlefield experiences, and now his education were all geared to that one goal, to serve God and to serve people. His dedication was complete. He would go where he was called to go, and do what he was called to do.

Chapter 23

❧❧

The Search Continues

There was considerable media coverage for the memorial service of the fallen hero Arthur Newman and the part he played in saving his brother. The newspapers in both Terre Haute and Charleston put the news on the front page when Art's remains were returned to Terre Haute for burial. This was important, and one of the things William had wanted to accomplish.

Because of the Coles County connection, the Charleston paper also ran a feature on the birth mother and the adoptive parents. The reporter researching the story had interviewed the judge who had finalized the adoption. He asked the judge what he remembered about that event of almost twenty years ago. The judge told him that the adoption record was permanently sealed. However; he was happy in this instance, that both sets of parents had the chance to honor this fine young man who was indeed a hero. He had not only saved his own brother but many others. He reminded the reporter that the young man had received the Silver Star with Clusters, which meant multiple awards of bravery. Quoting the Judge: "The secrecy in this case has been lifted by the adoptive parents and the birth mother by their own choice. I am very happy that the story of this young man could be openly reported, by Mrs. Trapp and the Wainrights, for the people of Coles County to read. The life of this young man was exemplary."

This story ran in the local paper, and this was how Orville learned the fate of his son. He wasn't very happy that he was left out, but knew he didn't deserve better. To the average reader, it was a heart-warming story, even though a tragic loss for the parents involved. That boy had spent years in this area and would undoubtedly be remembered for a long time. World War II was still very fresh in everyone's mind, and thousands of veterans could relate to what this young man represented.

Willis was reading the article again when something clicked in his head. He reread the judge's statement once again. He thought it curious that the judge used the wrong name for the adoptive parents. Didn't he mean the Newman's? Why did he make that error? No one else commented on it, so he assumed they hadn't noticed. Willis had a growing suspicion that he needed to check out. He was sure he wouldn't rest well until he did. He was personally acquainted with Judge Lewis, and maybe he could just talk to him about it. The Charleston paper apparently was not read in Indiana, because no one from the Newman family ever questioned it.

The military portion of the service for Art was solemn and short, but the guest speakers had plenty to say about Corporal Arthur Newman. William officiated at the service at the request of the Newman's. He painted a portrait of the young man who had made the ultimate sacrifice for his fellow man. During the service, Frances sat arm in arm with Mrs. Newman in the front row, and they drew on each other for strength. Later they would share their son with each other, as they truly recognized the treasure they had both known and loved.

The ride home was very quiet and Willis was deep in thought most of the time. They all were. Willis was thinking that his sister had plenty on her mind right now. Maybe in a few days he could share more with her. The reuniting of the mother with her son William had been very positive, and the relationship that developed between Frances and the Newman's was also very encouraging. Maybe there could be more.

Willis approached Judge Lewis rather casually. He explained to him that it was his four nephews that had been adopted back in the early thirties and knew the judge had officiated over each one. He appreciated his comments to the paper about the one who had died a hero, and it had meant a lot to the family to be able to share that story with the people. The judge agreed it was a very positive thing. When Willis continued talking about the other boys, he seemed a little defensive. The judge explained that all the information was forever sealed, but it had been obvious to him that all concerned were sharing in these special circumstances. Willis assured him that he agreed. Willis also added that the war had changed a lot of things and that these were different times. Who really knew what had happened to the others? Their fate might have been just like Arts. The judge listened to Willis, wondering what he was leading up to. Finally Willis asked him straight out, "Can't you check these things out and let my sister know?" The judge tensed at this suggestion and quickly responded that this was completely out of the question. Willis then said, "We already know about the Watsons, the Wainrights, and the Newmans. It isn't much of a secret anymore." The judge seemed momentarily flustered and asked how Willis had gotten those names. Willis just said he wished they had the fourth family also, but understood that the judge was bound by his ethics. The judge dismissed him by saying, "You're right about that. That name won't come from me," and walked away. Willis's ploy had worked, and now he knew there was more detective work to be done.

One avenue might be to see if there was any kind of register in existence at the children's home where a Mr. or Mrs. Wainright had visited anytime in the early 30's. If not, maybe they had registered in a local hotel or someone might remember the name for some reason. Adoptions didn't normally happen overnight and, if this Wainright family didn't live in the local area, then they had to stay somewhere. He'd go to work on that soon, but in the meantime he wouldn't tell Frances he had a lead. No need to get her hopes up because this could take a while.

Chapter 24

കൈ

Ted's Story

Audie's questions had triggered Ted's curiosity, and on his next visit home he sat down with his mother and told her of his conversation with his friend. Could she expand any more on information of his birth mother? She was amused at the book idea and half jokingly said, "Maybe Audie will play you. You look enough alike. Maybe he's your brother." Ted laughed with her, but pressed her to tell him how they did come to adopt him and the procedures they had followed.

She sat down with her knitting and proceeded to tell him their story. She'd been an only child of a military family and had met his father when her family was stationed at Fort Sill, Oklahoma. They fell in love and married. In their first ten years, his father had two tours in the Philippines while she remained at home with her parents. They had wanted a family right away but weren't having any luck. After ten years they finally had gone to Chicago to a specialist to find out why they couldn't have children. Of course, they were disappointed when it was determined that they never would. After spending a few days in Chicago, they caught a train south hoping to vacation in New Orleans before returning to their next post. They were near central Illinois when a major derailment ahead of them caused the tracks to be impassable, and they were stranded for a time in a town called Mattoon. They checked into the local hotel to wait until the rails were fixed. There they met a couple over dinner. The couple was from St. Louis and was staying there also. They seemed to enjoy the younger couple and insisted on buying dinner for a man in uniform and his wife.

Their story was that, they were staying at the hotel until the judge in the neighboring town had time to finalize an adoption for them. They had wanted to stay close in case there were any last minute snags. The woman went on to explain about the dying mother who had given four boys up for adoption and the county was trying to find homes for them. Ted's mother had confided in them that they had already been discussing the possibility of adopting, and what they were hearing had really gotten their attention. They had many questions for the pair. The couple suggested that they might even get preferential treatment by being military. If they were interested, perhaps they could put in a good word for them and introduce them to the attorney they were using. This could minimize background checks and other requirements and speed up the process. They told Ted's parents that they thought they would make fine candidates. "We contacted the home and put our application in the next day, and we've never regretted that decision for a minute," his mother said. "We missed a couple of trains, but when we left Mattoon a week later, you were with us. That wreck must have been fate working for us. Of course, we never made it to New Orleans." Ted asked, "Who was the couple you talked to?" "I've tried to remember that name many times because I would have loved to thank them, but I can't. His name was Charles and hers was Kathryn, but other than that we can't remember. About the only other thing I remember about that whirlwind week is that you were a brave little boy, and you loved the train ride. Not much for a feature film," she chuckled.

Chapter 25

৯৯ ৺৶

Coming Together

It was a much different life for Frances after her dad died and she had moved to town. Her days were spent making shoes and her evenings with her mother. They went to church three times a week, and she and her mother prayed regularly for the missing boys in their lives. She didn't grieve over them daily, but not knowing anything about them was difficult. She wondered more about Ted, the younger one than she did about Leo. She thought that Leo, being the older, would have been better able to cope with the change. Ted was uprooted so young before he really had a chance to know family. It's possible that he didn't have any memories of them. Also, Eddie was more of a concern now. He'd been gone for three years, and his letters were few and far between. He seemed to have taken a liking to Colorado, though he had never made it as far as Denver to see his Uncle, as far as she knew. At least she knew where he was and could write him.

It had been three years since she had gone to Terre Haute and met the Newman's for Art's ceremony. This had meant so much to her, and she still marveled at the life Art had lived. If only she could bring him back, but she would have to live with the memory. Many mothers were thankful to have their sons back because of him, whether they knew him by name or not. God had preserved William's life by using Art, and now look what he is doing with his life. "The Lord be praised," she uttered to herself. Both William and Art's adoptive parents were to be highly commended, and she thanked the Lord for them. She prayed that Leo and Ted had been as fortunate.

She was standing over the sink finishing the supper dishes one evening when Willis walked in. He checked on his mother first, who was dozing in her chair, and came over to sit at the table. He didn't refuse the apple pie she offered, and Frances sat with him while he ate.

After sharing news of his family, he went on to say that he'd missed his calling. "I should have been an FBI man instead of a teacher," he said. Frances looked at him knowing he had something to tell her and wanting him to get on with it. He said, "Sit down, Fanny." He hadn't called her that since they were children, "I have a story to tell. Remember when the Gazette wrote the article on Art? Well, when they interviewed Judge Lewis he got confused and referred to Art's parents as the Wainrights." He had Frances' full attention now. "I talked to the judge, pretending that I knew more than I did about the adoptive parents. I thought he mistakenly gave the wrong parents' name to the press, based on his memory. I was sure enough about this that I've been doing detective work on and off for three years, and it has paid off. It's been a long, hard search but once I got started, I couldn't stop. That's why I should be working for J. Edgar Hoover." He paused long enough to get himself a glass of water at the sink. Frances said, "Willis, you get back over here, sit down, and tell me what you know. You can't leave me hanging like this."

Willis sat down and started his long narrative of the different things he'd been doing these past years. His attempt was to find the people the judge had referred to. The name was Wainright. There was no one in a three county area by that name, so he started trying to trace anyone by that name that might have visited Charleston back in 1931. All the adoption legal work was done in Charleston, so it stood to reason that the people had to be here at one time or another to finalize things. He'd gone out to the children's home and asked if they had some kind of logbook or registry that they had kept over the years. They said they did but that it wasn't open to the public. The boys coming through the home had the right to have their identity protected, and that record could only be obtained by court order. Willis said he explained to the manager that he wasn't interested in the boy's registry, just the guest one. He went back in storage and brought out two old books and put them on the desk. It turned out that they only went back ten years. The manager informed Willis that Mr. Kirkley, the previous superintendent, probably cleaned house when he retired. When he asked about his whereabouts, he was informed that he had died just the previous year down in Effingham. Willis felt he had hit a dead end.

He was discouraged and didn't pursue his next idea for several months. It was a long shot, but he figured that they had to stay somewhere during the adoption proceedings and that possibly it was in a local hotel. Being a college town, they had more than one hotel even back then. Willis' had the idea that a couple looking to adopt were probably able to afford the better accommodations, and that eliminated some of the seedier hotels, at least in his mind. He talked it over with friends, and their memories were of The Majestic Hotel downtown. One of his fellow teachers knew the operator over there, made inquiries, and found out that the hotel was required by law to keep registries. Finding them might be the trick. The manager was persuaded by his friend to look, and he said he would when time permitted. Willis had all but given up when, six months later, the manager uncovered a register for the years 1930 through 1933. Willis was allowed to go through it, and while he didn't find the name of Wainright, he did find some similar names that he thought worthwhile to check out. Some had addresses and some were illegible, so Willis tried to trace those that he could. He didn't have any success. After that experience, he just about gave up the search all together. He wasn't even inclined to go back and check out some of the less desirable local hotels.

It was months later when the topic came up over dinner when his son and his wife were visiting. His son's wife, Betsy, asked if he'd checked out Mattoon. She was from Mattoon, and her uncle owns the Royal Hotel there and had for years. Maybe Willis would want to check with him. "It might be worth a try," Willis said, "but I'm hitting a lot of dead ends." About three months later, Betsy asked him if he had pursued the idea and he hadn't. So she volunteered to help out. "What are you looking for?" she asked. Willis told her his idea was, that a man and wife named Wainright may have stayed overnight there in early 1931 while adopting one of the boys. Three weeks later she called

Willis and said she and her uncle had located a registry for that period. A Major and Mrs J. Wainright had indeed been there for four nights in 1931. Their address was Fort Benning, Georgia. Willis told Frances, "I couldn't believe what I was hearing. I was playing detective, but I guess I didn't really believe that I'd ever uncover anything this remote. And I wouldn't have except Betsy wouldn't let me stop. I guess I need to give her the credit." Frances said, "What happened then?" "This story goes on and on, Frances. Do you really have the time?" His humor didn't please her, and she threatened him. Willis said he didn't quite know what to do with the information he had.

What he had was a man in the military twenty years ago, a world war since, and now a conflict in Korea, with an address of Fort Benning, Georgia. How could he make something of all this? If the man was a Major in 1931 and not too old to adopt, how old a man would he be today? Eisenhower had been a Major in 1939, and now he'd been elected President. This man had to be getting old, according to Willis' logic.

He told Frances that the name Wainright did have a familiar ring to it, but it took a while to zero in on it. He was reading about General Douglas MacArthur one day and he almost jumped out of his chair when he came across the name General Jonathon Wainwright. He had called to his wife and did a jig around the chair. Could they have been this lucky? He read on and discovered that this was the general who had surrendered the Philippines to the Japanese and had spent the rest of the war in a prison camp. There was also a picture of the signing of the unconditional surrender by the Japanese on the USS Missouri. There in attendance, as big as life, was an emaciated General Jonathon Wainwright. He felt sure that, not only had he found the man, but a famous man to boot. This was a famous man that would be easily traceable even today. He read that this man had received the Medal of Valor from President Truman and is a personal friend of MacArthur. His nickname was Skinny Wainwright, and Willis wondered if he was always that thin or was it just after the years in the prison camps. As he read on, he was sure that this was the man. His wife wasn't sure though. She noticed that in his notes he had written Major and Mrs. J. Wainright. In the biography of MacArthur, the spelling was Jonathon Wainwright. Could that make a difference? Willis didn't think it really did. His daughter-in-law probably just made an error in copying the name, but he would check it out to be sure. He called Betsy and asked if she would mind just double-checking that registry entry at the hotel just one more time. The question was the precise spelling of the name. It was a couple of days later when Betsy called and confirmed that the name in the registry definitely did not have a second W in the name. This sent Willis scurrying to get more information on General Jonathon Wainwright, which was available in the newspaper archives. It showed that the general was born in 1883, which meant he was forty-eight years old in 1931. Possible, but his doubt was slowly building. That's pretty old for adoption. He had thought he'd better not go off the deep end yet and say anything to his sister. The Wainwright's had long and distinguished careers in the military dating back before the Civil War, and it would have been nice to think that Ted had ended up in such a family. Caution told him to go slow. It was looking less likely all the time.

It was then he received a call from his daughter-in-law who had made a startling discovery. Her Uncle, who had helped in the search, was talking to friends at the Kiwanis one day about his niece's involvement in a search for an adopted boy. He dropped the name of Wainright into the conversation. One of his friends quickly picked up on this familiar but also unusual name. This man mentioned that his son had graduated from VMI in the summer of 1949 and that he had attended the graduation and met the commandant, General James Wainright. Was he sure the name didn't have a second W, as in Jonathon Wainwright? The man said he was sure but he'd double check. A phone call to his son settled that question by his looking at the signature on his diploma. There was no second W. The Virginia Military Institute in Lexington, Virginia, in 1949. Now that was a lead he could pursue.

A call to the Virginia Historical Society confirmed that Gen. Wainright was still the commandant. He was born in 1900, married a Jennifer Walls in 1922, and had one son named Theodore who was born in 1925. Now he was sure and couldn't wait to tell his sister, and here he was. "This is what I know, and I believe it is accurate. I've come to you today with a search for Ted completed. I know I can trust you not to do anything foolish with this information, but what you do is up to you." Frances said, "First I'll share it with William. Then we'll decide what to do and when to do it." After Willis left she shared the information with her mother. Frances was relieved to know that Ted was apparently alive and well and that the war had not claimed another of her sons. But, she didn't know what she was going to do about it. She didn't want to act on emotion and get anyone hurt.

Chapter 26

❦

William And The
Prodigal Son

Ted had graduated with honors in 1950 from the Academy, but his former roommate Joe had been at the top of the class. Both of them asked for and got their preferred assignments. Ted was assigned to Fort Belvoir, Virginia. This Fort, just outside of D.C., was close to the heartbeat of the military, the Pentagon, but it was also within easy driving distance of Donna. She was finishing her junior year of college, majoring in education. While they had remained close over the years, Ted could not convince her to make it exclusive, meaning no other guys or gals. Now perhaps he could woo her in a way he couldn't while a cadet. She had always said that being an army wife was not the ideal for her, but Ted had plans to change her mind. The growing conflict in Korea wasn't going to help his cause much, but he had to try.

By an act of Congress he had been commissioned a First Lieutenant at graduation in deference to his rank and record in WWII, so he had a jump-start on his classmates at the Point, including Joe. He didn't know whether his father had anything to do with it, but it didn't seem illogical for him to get some credit for his active duty during the war. After all, he'd been a First Lieutenant soon after D-Day.

He was in Richmond for Donna's graduation in 1951, and to his surprise, Joe was there too. He had not seen him since graduation, and the three of them had a lot of catching up to do. When they were alone, Joe told him he had asked for Korean duty and would soon be flying to Japan. Ted understood what Joe was doing but didn't feel compelled to do so himself. He had seen war and he could wait. He'd go when called on, but this time he wasn't volunteering. Ted had been transferred to the Pentagon and was in line for his Captain's bars. He was working on war plans for the Korean conflict.

Joe had one other thing he wanted to talk to Ted about. He'd invited Donna to Fort Benning for a weekend, and she had agreed to come. This set Ted back a little. He knew Donna dated, but this was the first indication that one of her beaus was Joe. He was more than a little hurt and angry with both of them, and told her so the next day when they met. She told Ted, with more than a little fire in her own eyes, that she would see whom she wanted when she wanted. Ted knew then that perhaps he had better not put all his eggs in one basket and to start playing the field himself. After four years of investing his time and effort in this little belle, it looked like he had lost.

Eighteen months later, Joe was back from Korea and had asked Captain Ted Wainright to be his best man in his marriage to Donna. Things had been stormy at times and he had some growing up to do, but these two people were still his best friends. He finally got the little Virginia belle out of his system, had met someone special himself, and now he could be happy for the two of them. Joe had told him, "You may outrank me, but I'm still the top of our class. Just ask Donna." Ted knew he was cured when he could laugh at this. He and his fiancée would be there on Joe and Donna's special day.

William was serving in his first church at Falls Church, Virginia. Upon graduation from seminary he had numerous opportunities to serve with offers from colleges, foreign missions, to large congregations, but after much prayer decided on the senior pastor position in Falls Church. One day he got an unexpected call from his Uncle Willis. His initial reaction when the secretary announced the call, was that someone was sick or dying. He was relieved when Willis exchanged a few pleasantries before he got to the point of his call. He initially asked, "Would you like to locate your brother Ted?" William responded in the affirmative almost immediately. He had thought very much about it from time to time, especially after knowing Art's fate. He hadn't obsessed over it because of the uncertainty of relationships. His being reunited with his family had worked out well, but one could never be sure that it was the right thing for others. He told Willis, "In the right circumstances I would, but let's travel easy on this one until we know if Ted wants to know his birth family." It was a long conversation as Willis filled him in on the details, and the story had the minister on the edge of his chair in anticipation. When Willis ended, William could only say, "Wow, you are a sleuth, aren't you? Does my mother know about this?" Willis said she had known for sometime but had been patient to protect Ted's privacy and his family life. Finally she had asked Willis to call William for her and get his advice.

Willis went on to say that the time seemed right when they learned William had taken a church in Virginia and could be in the position to get a closer look at the situation. His sister would rely totally on William's evaluation of what to do, or not do, next. William said, "I'm glad you called. Give me some time to think this over and I'll be talking to you when I have reached a decision." As soon as he hung up he knew that he'd be making a trip. He had heard Virginia was a beautiful state, and it was time for him to check it out for himself. He wrote a note on his calendar pad to tell the secretary he'd be out of town the Friday and Saturday of the second week in June. His note to himself was, "Gone Fishing."

VMI was in a beautiful setting, the rolling hills of Virginia. Its walls were steeped in the history of the men who had roamed the halls and gone on to distinguish themselves in the service of their country. One fact caught William's eye, and that was of the hundreds of VMI graduates who had served in the Civil War: only a handful, less than ten, had served on the Union side. There was no doubt he was in Confederate country. It had a wonderful reputation as a learning institution and training ground for young men, and William was eager to check out its commandant. A little research had filled him in on a few relevant facts.

The campus was quite this second Friday in June as he slowly walked from where he had parked in the lot. The big house was no doubt the commandant's, and it had beautiful gardens all around it. He asked a young man in uniform where he could find General Wainright and was directed to a newer building where the general had his office. He approached it with some apprehension and went up the steps to the door. He knew he might come out more quickly than he was going in, but in his heart he knew this man didn't get where he was by making rash decisions. He didn't normally wear a clerical collar but was glad he had his on this trip. It might help. At the information desk, he was directed up the steps to the rear offices where another cadet sat. He introduced himself and asked to see General Wainright. The general was in, and he was told to have a seat and he'd be out to greet him shortly.

Soon a distinguished man in his late fifties came out, shook his hand and invited him into the inner office. He had on a business suit and smiled as he greeted William, asking him if this was his first visit to VMI. William said it was. William opened by saying he was pastor of a church in Falls Church, although he was originally from Missouri. He had driven down this Friday to see the beautiful campus but also to discuss what might be a delicate topic with him. He wanted to assure the general that he was just introducing the subject and it would halt immediately if it was a topic that he was not comfortable or interested in discussing. He wasn't here to cause problems for anyone. The general didn't hesitate to tell William to continue. It was obvious he was confident that he could control any situation that might arise. Williams's next words did surprise him however, when William got directly to the point by saying, "I believe that I am your son's brother." The general just looked at him for about fifteen seconds and replied, "You don't look anything like him. What makes you think you are?" William relayed quickly his own background and his own adoption from the children's home in Charleston, Illinois. He didn't have to go further because the General said, "This is wonderful. What a wonderful surprise. We knew Ted had three brothers, but they were gone when we arrived on the scene, and I can't imagine a better present for my son than to re-introduce him to his big brother. We never had any other children, so he's always been an only child and I'm sure he will be delighted. Can you also tell me about the others?"

Frankly, William was surprised at the immediate acceptance. He didn't think he was going to have any problem getting information for Frances, but knew he'd best not get into that at this point until he became better acquainted. The general asked William to come and go with him. He told the cadet at the desk that he would be gone for a while, and if anyone called could be found at the mansion. As they walked along, William gave the general a brief run down on Ted's other brothers. The general listened intently as he guided him to the house and explained he probably should have prepared his wife a little. "She's busy making something for her friend's daughter's wedding tomorrow. On top of that we're expecting Ted home this very afternoon. I got excited and didn't get her called. She's not going to believe what we're about to tell her."

They walked into the house and the general went to a door leading into a large dining room obviously used for dinner parties. There, seated at the table with materials spread all about was an attractive woman who looked up as they entered. The general walked over to her and, taking her by the hands, pulled her to her feet, saying, "Hold on, darling. You're about to meet Ted's brother." Her hand flew to her mouth in surprise, and then a little puzzlement shown in her eyes. Her husband told her, "This is the Reverend William Watson of Falls Church. He has wonderful news for our son, and for us." He then in rapid-fire fashion gave her the information that William had revealed to him, ending with, "I can't think of a better surprise for Ted when he gets here today." Mrs. Wainright then approached William with her hand out and invited him into the parlor where they could sit and talk. She first led him about the room, showing him pictures on the tables of first a young soldier in full uniform, the same young man in what appeared to be a cadet's uniform, and then one of him in civilian clothes with his arm around a petite, pretty young lady. She said, "This is your brother. Does he look like what you remembered?" William said, I'd know him anywhere," which was only a little fib.

They quickly exchanged stories and information and the time passed so quickly that Mrs. Wainright finally had to call a recess. "We're have a timing problem here and, if I could make a suggestion, let's do this. Ted's due about four this afternoon with his fiancée whom we have never met and they'll be staying here for the weekend. The problem is, Ted is going to want us to get acquainted with his fiancée this afternoon. The second problem is that Ted is best man for a wedding tomorrow, and all kind of activities are planned for this evening. Today will be all about best man duties and rehearsal dinners and Ted's fiancée, and I don't want this to come out until we have enough time to deal with it properly. My idea, if you agree, is for you to stay over as our houseguest. We'll introduce you as an ex army chaplain and friend. When things are less hectic, possibly tomorrow, we'll tell the whole truth. What do you think?" William smiled, "Well, it's not exactly a lie. I was a chaplain during the war, and it would be nice to have the time we need to get re-acquainted. One limitation, I need to be back in Falls Church Sunday morning in the pulpit."

They all agreed that this was the plan and Mrs. Wainright called the maid to show William to a room. "That's one good thing about these old mansions, they have plenty of bedrooms. It's summer so you won't notice the draft. Please excuse me for now, I just have to get back to those bridesmaids hats. Just make yourself at home, and yes, this is a lovely surprise." The general had a young cadet bring William's car to the mansion so he could have his overnight bag.

William had just unpacked and was stretching out on the old fashioned bed when someone rapped on the door and announced lunch. He glanced at his watch, twelve-thirty, another three hours before he saw that little dark-eyed boy of his youth. He could hardly contain his excitement. Having lost Art made this meeting so important. He wished his mother Frances could be here, but maybe one day soon she will be. Ted, a war veteran, a West Point graduate, and he would be meeting him under a pretense that was going to feel very strange.

He hoped that Ted would respond as well as his folks had. He hesitated for a moment in deciding whether to wear the collar again and concluded that he probably should. He might need all the props he could muster to get through these next hours and play out the charade they had planned. At least it would give him a chance to observe Ted before things got emotional.

After lunch he walked around the campus again with the general. Ted's father explained some of the special memorials and their significance. The main thing that he wanted to talk about, though, was Art's story. This was the thing legends were made of, the general believed. Especially since he had in fact saved his brother William's life unknowingly. He thought the nation needed to hear this story, even if it was eight years old. The general was moved when William mentioned the astonishing resemblance between Ted and Art. He told the general he would be happy to put him in contact with the Newman's, Art's family.

They also talked about the European war and the action Ted had seen on D-Day and afterward. By comparing details, it became evident that William and Ted were in the same general area and their paths could have crossed. Ted's final posting at Nuremberg coincided perfectly with a short time William had spent there at the end of the war.

William questioned the General about his service in the South Pacific, and the coincidence of the similarity of his name to General Jonathon Wainwright of the Philippine's campaign. The General said that this did create some confusion from time to time when people learned he was on MacArthur's staff. But it had not been a problem after the war because Jonathon had become better known and a household name after receiving the Presidential Medal of Valor. He had never met the man personally. He was on his way home when Mac and Skinny got together on the USS Missouri.

The time slipped past quickly and they saw a convertible with its top down headed toward the mansion. "Guess we'd better get back," the General said. "I see a certain young man and his fiancée have arrived." They walked swiftly down the quadrangle. William felt his heart racing.

Ted had met Joyce at church, which was unusual since Ted had not been a regular churchgoer. Under the circumstances, though, it was understandable because he had been attending the wedding of a fellow officer at the post. Joyce was one of the bridesmaids, and when she marched down the aisle with her beautiful red hair, Ted's heart stood at attention. He'd had a rough six months getting over Donna and wanted to move on, and maybe he'd just seen the moving squad that would do the job. None of the friends he was sitting with knew whether she was engaged or married, but he didn't wait for an invitation at the reception. He moved right in and took matters into his own hands.

As it happened, she was unattached and the chemistry was right. It had been a whirlwind courtship and he couldn't stand to have a day pass without seeing her. They had so much in common. It didn't take him long to pop the question and make plans to take her home to meet the parents. He had met her mother and father the week before and now she was going to meet these very special people in his life. As they drove through the campus toward the mansion, he was in high spirits. She seemed radiant and happy, although windblown. The last fifty miles had been with the top down. He knew his parents were going to love this girl and felt so fortunate that she had come into his life. Maybe she was reason enough to go to church more often, he had jokingly told her. She had told him, in no uncertain terms, that she was a churchgoing gal and wasn't planning on going alone, so get accustomed to it. They were the same age, had great families, and Ted just couldn't believe his luck.

They were almost to the door when his mother came out to greet them. They were standing there when his father walked up the walk with a man Ted didn't know, obviously a priest. Tall and dark, he didn't look like a priest except for the collar. Ted introduced Joyce to his father, and could immediately tell that he was impressed with what he saw. His father in turn introduced a friend, the Reverend William Watson, who had been a chaplain in the Army during the war. They shook hands, and Ted thought the chaplain seemed pretty intense in his scrutiny of him, but maybe it was just his imagination. They went inside where the emphasis shifted back to the Ted's fiancée and the ring and the big plans they were making. Ted explained to his folks that Joyce was from Arlington, and her father was also retired military. William sat quietly in the background and watched all of this, trying to see the little boy he had carried around on his back. Ted had come a long way, and this confident young man was a lot of fun to watch. He could hardly wait until they could talk on a truly personal level.

The whole evening was crammed with activities, with people coming and going. During the course of the evening, William met Joe, the groom to be. William excused himself early, saying he had something pressing that he needed to take care of. Fortunately he'd brought his outline for his Sunday's sermon, and he took this time to study it and review scripture for it. He also took the time to call Illinois, when Ted and Joyce were out, and gave Frances an update on where he was and what he was doing. "You will be most proud of this young man," he assured her. "I'm just beginning to know who he is, but I can tell you for sure that he has a family who loves him very much. I'll contact you next week with more." Ted was a dynamo, always energized and on the move, much like he remembered him being as a six year old. He did resemble the adult pictures of Art that the Newman's had shown him, and he hoped he would have an opportunity to take some snapshots of him before returning home.

The morning had been as equally frantic, and William didn't actually see Ted and Joyce until they were headed out the door to the wedding. He accompanied the Wainrights to the ceremony and it was beautiful. But, at the reception, William was beginning to wonder if he's get his opportunity to talk to Ted before he had leave for Falls Church.

The reception was huge and had gone on for what seemed hours when the general dragged his son and Joyce over to where they were sitting. He said, "Ted, William has to return home this evening, and we haven't been entirely honest about him. Sit a moment while we level with you." Ted looked a little puzzled and looked over at Joyce who shrugged her shoulders. The general continued, "William here was a chaplain in the Army during the war, but more than that, he is your brother." The announcement almost made Ted tip his chair over backwards. As he struggled to regain his balance, he said, "And you kept this secret from me all these years! Why?" His mother's eyebrows furrowed briefly, and she looked stunned. Then she broke into a laugh. "No, silly. Not a stepbrother. He's your brother." That didn't lessen the shock any for Ted as he sat and looked at William, but slowly the recognition came. When it did, he literally dived across the table into William's arms. People at the surrounding tables weren't sure what was happening but could see that there were tears involved and a lot of hugging, so they guessed it was okay.

They hardly made a dent in all they wanted to talk about before William had to leave. They made plans to meet the following week. They were almost neighbors. On his way home William felt blessed for what he had experienced these past two days, but knew he'd need another blessing if he were going to do what he needed to do in the pulpit later this day. It was already past midnight.

Chapter 27

ॐ ॐ

The Final Search

It was New Year's Day, 1960. Frances was sitting by the fire with her feet up and in pain. She hated taking painkillers because they bothered her stomach, but she might have to. It had been three years since her mother had died and she still missed her very much. She was lonely. She had been forced to take disability retirement the previous year, but she had survived tougher tasks before and would get through this, too. Her mom had left her the home and it was paid for, so it didn't take much for her to get by. Besides, her son William had been so generous to her over the years. She got to see him about twice a year and was hopeful that he would get a chance to visit again before long. She had been so happy when he found a wife, and the one he married was exceptional. He and Molly, Art's friend, had met at the memorial for Art back in 1948 and had kept in touch over the years. They had a warm relationship, but it was years before any romance developed. When it did, it was special. They had married in his church in Falls Church in 1956, and Frances had been there along with Ted and Mr. and Mrs. Newman. He had waited until he was thirty-five, but truly the Lord blessed him again. Molly normally came with him when he visited, and last year she got to meet her newest granddaughter. They had named her Ursey.

Ted didn't make it as often. He had been stationed abroad for two of the last four years. She would never forget that wonderful reunion that she had with him. He and William had come all the way from Virginia and spent three days with her and they relived all the old memories. He was very successful as a soldier, having been promoted to the rank of Colonel just last year. At last notice he was back at the Pentagon again. He did make Frances' mothers funeral, but she would only get an occasional letter from him or his wife. They had two children now and were very busy.

Eddie had married a nice girl in Colorado and was making his home there. They came home soon after the marriage and spent a week in Charleston, and she got to know her new daughter-in-law Barbara. She'd be a good influence on him. He brought news of his Uncle Robert and his family, and they had made plans to get together from time to time. Eddie had invested in a small business and he and Barbara were struggling to make it a success.

She was sitting there thinking of all this when there was a knock on the door. She didn't feel like moving, so she just called out and said, "Come on in, it's not locked." It was Uncle Adren, which surprised her; he just normally walked on in without knocking. She enjoyed his visits but thought it strange that he would be here on New Year's Day. Uncle Adren had some tough years, having lost his wife nearly ten years ago, but he was still the best at visiting family and helping out when needed. He had a habit of just making the "rounds" and dropping by once in a while. She knew her mother and aunts had appreciated him more and more as they got older. He was kind of the glue that held the family together as he visited all of them.

"Is there any coffee over there?" he asked, pointing to the kitchen. "Help yourself. There might be a piece of pie if you want to help yourself." Uncle Adren liked pies. He sat down with her, making small talk and inquiring of her health. Only then did he get a little serious and got into the reason for the visit. "I heard something and it's taken me a while to finally decide to tell you about it," he said. "I hope you don't make me regret passing this along, and I'm not even sure what you can do about it anyway."

He began this story about what was said at the Whitford Reunion, held in Paris, Illinois, in August. Frances had missed that one. He and his brother Jesse had been discussing Frances' health when Jesse told Adren about something that had happened on his job some time past. He worked for the Secretary of State in Springfield at the time. His job was working in personnel, and he was responsible for screening applications for employment. They were expanding the Licensing Stations throughout the state and were searching for qualified personnel. Of course, one of the key qualifications was for the applicant to be a republican. The Rockford area was growing rapidly and there was a key job opening there. Jesse had narrowed the applicants down to about a half dozen and was checking references before he forwarded his recommendations on to the Secretary.

One application in particular caught his attention as he read the detailed background. A Leo Swenson, formerly of Mendota, Illinois. His background was rather routine, a war veteran and a dairy farmer who had a business college diploma earned under the GI Bill. What caught his eye, though, was his place of birth: Coles County, Illinois. In the applicant's comments, the man mentioned he had been adopted at age eleven by the Swenson's, had attended high school in Mendota, was a Pearl Harbor survivor, and was given an honorable discharge with the rank of Chief Petty Officer. Other work experience was listed and he had a wife and two children. A phone call confirmed that he was a registered republican.

Jesse didn't know very much about Frances and Orville's troubles, but his wife did remember that one of the children was named Leo. From this he concluded that there just might be a connection, and the man was about the right age. He felt strongly enough there was a connection that he made sure the man got the job, but he never actually met the man. He'd considered telling Adren about it before but had forgotten about it. In fact, he had forgotten it until just that day when the subject of Frances' health came up. "Jesse, she's only been looking for her four boys for thirty years," Adren had told him and he just shrugged. He didn't know. "That's about all I can tell you about that. Apparently that was at least five years ago," Adren said. Frances tried to control the emotions she was feeling at that moment. Her oldest son had been alive and well just a few years ago, but she wasn't doing very well herself. What was she going to do with the information? She tried to mask her thoughts by asking about Adren's family and getting an update on them. They were pretty well scattered to the four winds, but he did mention his youngest who lived in Rockford. That fact didn't escape her. She thanked him for coming by as he got up to leave. She could always depend on Uncle Adren.

Willis attended the reunions regularly, so that afternoon when he checked in, she asked the names of Adren's children. He couldn't remember them all, but he knew the ones she didn't. She made a mental note of the youngest named Dale. Now she needed to figure out what to do about it.

Chapter 28

❧❦

Final Link

Leo had bounced around for quite awhile after the war, and among other things, helped his dad expand his dairy herd. He also sold cars to returning veterans, and living at home he had built up a little nest egg of his own. After talking to other vets, he decided to go over to DeKalb to the university and take advantage of the GI Bill education package. They offered four-year degree programs, but at his age he was more interested in the two-year business course. With that diploma he was able to get a job in the office of an industry in Rockford, and soon after met his future wife Carol. She worked until their daughter was born and then quit to be a full-time homemaker. Their home life was more important to Leo than the extra money she could have made.

Eventually they were able to buy a modest home on the north side of Rockford and were very happy when their son, whom they named William, came along. Leo had told his wife about his early life and why there had to be a William, but he never intended to get into that with their family. They had grandparents here, and that was more important. No need to confuse them with ancient history. Their children were very special to his parents, and he smiled at the way they doted on their grand kids. They had never been that way with him, but that was okay. His parents would always have his love and respect for what they did for him, and his loyalty.

He had applied for the job at the State of Illinois Licensing Bureau because of the benefits it offered, and because at the time he was disillusioned with his job. He'd been passed over for promotions a couple of times for men who had four-year degrees, and he thought he was better qualified. He knew getting the job would be a long shot; but nothing ventured, nothing gained. He was a precinct committeeman but had not been that fervent a politician, and he was sure there were many other applicants with stronger party affiliations. He did get the interview, however, and went with rather low expectations and was very surprised when he was hired. His new supervisor only said, "You've got clout," and he had no idea what he meant.

He had been on the job about five years. After dinner one evening, he was elected babysitter so his wife could go out and play cards. They weren't babies anymore; in fact, they had a card game of their own that lasted until bedtime. They had just gotten to sleep when the phone rang. The voice on the other end said, "Is this Leo Swenson?" He said it was, and the voice continued, "You don't know me but my name is Dale Whitford, a first cousin of your mother Frances Trapp." The voice paused and, when Leo said nothing, continued, "She asked me to contact you and introduce myself. I live here in Rockford now. You may remember my father Adren, your mother's uncle." Leo was shaken. The only thing he could say was, "This isn't a good time right now. I'll get back to you. You're in the book, aren't you?" Dale was rather surprised at the abruptness but said that he was. Leo hung up.

Afterward Dale reconsidered and thought maybe Leo's reaction wasn't that unusual. Who knows what the man was doing on the other end of the phone line. He'd just have to wait a day or two to respond to Frances' letter that he had gotten the previous week. Dale was surprised to receive such a letter.

He remembered Frances, but their acquaintance was pretty much restricted to reunions and information that his dad had passed on to him. She was at least his dad's age. In her letter she had mentioned her son Leo, and went on to explain that in the thirties she had been forced to give him up for adoption. She had gone through some tough times and had no other choice due to her health. Leo now lived in Rockford, and she thought it would be nice if Dale would contact him and get

148

acquainted. His adopted name was Leo Swenson, and she felt Dale would not have any problem locating him in the phone book. She was sure Leo would like to get to know more of his family, and being from Coles County gave Dale and Leo something in common.

She went on to say that she had also given up three other boys but had since located them, and slowly but surely they were getting reacquainted. Later on Dale found out this was only part of the truth, but at the time it didn't put up any warning flags for him. Leo was a first cousin once removed, and he was looking forward to getting acquainted. Dale and his wife didn't know that many people in Rockford themselves.

What he didn't know was that Frances had called Leo's house twice already. After identifying herself to Leo, he had hung up on her, both times. In her letter to Dale, she had also included the names and addresses of two of her other boys. She thought perhaps Dale would like to get acquainted with them also. Both were out east, so Dale thought that could wait until a later time.

The evening after the call, Dale and his wife were at home in their apartment when the doorbell rang. Dale got up to answer it and was confronted by a stern looking man in a dark suit. The man identified himself as Leo Swenson. Dale offered him his hand, but instead the man stepped inside, passed him, and stood in the middle of the room. Dale closed the door unsure of what to think, when Leo said, "If you're here trying to cause a problem for me and my family, I won't stand for it." He was intimidating for a guy about five foot five and twenty years older than he. But Dale said, "Whoa here, maybe I'd better know what's going on before you start with the threats. Sit down and tell me what's on your mind."

Leo sat down on the edge of a chair and started, "I haven't seen my birth mother in nearly thirty years. Then she starts calling me out of the blue and has you calling me. She isn't part of my life anymore, and my children don't even know that I'm adopted. They have grandparents here and that's the way it's going to stay. Also, my parents are still living, and I'll not have them hurt by some interference at this time in their lives." Dale listened and immediately apologized. "I didn't know any of this was happening. I was just going by her letter to me and had no idea of the real situation. I would never want to create problems of any kind. Maybe the letter will help explain where I'm coming from." He walked to a desk, picked up an envelope, and handed it to Leo. Leo took the letter out of the envelope and read it. He was quiet for a minute and then told Dale, "I'm sorry I've been so ugly. I rushed to judgment and should have discussed it with you first. It's just that the stakes are so high." Dale assured him that it was very understandable and that he need not feel bad. Leo indicated that this information about his brothers was something else and he'd have to think more about that. He asked Dale if he could keep the letter. Leo handed back the envelope with Frances' address on it. With that, Leo rose, shook Dale's hand, and apologized again to Dale's wife and left.

Dale and his wife were in a daze, thinking this was an incident that they probably would never forget. It just so happened that they had an adoption pending of their own, and only a few months later were the parents of a baby boy. They would never withhold any details of his adoption from him, and prayed that he would always feel free to discuss it with them. Secrecy could be a bad thing.

Dale didn't contact Frances, but rather filled his dad in on what had happened. Only a few days later, he had a note from Frances. It read, "Your dad stopped by today and read me the riot act. I deserved it. I not only mislead you, but I betrayed his trust. Please forgive me for getting you caught up in the middle of things. I can only say that I have been quite ill, and am desperate after all these years to pull my family back together before it's too late. I didn't consult my other sons before I tried these drastic tactics. I'm sure neither of them would have gone along with it. It won't happen again. One last favor; if Leo should ever contact you please apologize for me. Tell him that I hope he doesn't harbor ill feelings or feel that I betrayed him in any way thirty years ago. They told me I was dying, and I insisted they all be adopted together, but my wishes were not carried out. I got to say goodbye to William, Art, and Ted. There was this one thing that I didn't get to say to Leo. If we never meet again this side of heaven, we'll meet on that beautiful shore. God bless you. I wish only the best for you." Dale's dad called a month later to say Frances had died in her sleep.

As Frances was dying, William and Ted joined Eddy at her bedside. She smiled at each of them in turn and whispered, "I love you. I'm so proud of all of you, and I know I've been blessed. I'm a forgiven sinner, and I pray that one day we'll all be reunited on that beautiful shore." Those were the last words that she spoke, and that night she peacefully passed.

Chapter 29

৯~৶

The Circle Is Closed

After his visit with Dale, Leo couldn't help but spend considerable time thinking about this woman who had given him birth. She was a warm and loving mother who had never given up on finding him. Although he didn't know or understand all the circumstances leading up to her giving him up for adoption, he still remembered the woman and knew in his heart that she didn't do it without a battle.

As a youth, he had felt some anger and resentment for what she had done; but now as an adult and a father himself, he understood that things could happen. He bore her genes and knew that she did everything she could, just like he would have. His memory and thoughts of his dad were not so generous. It was his mother who had instilled values in him and introduced him to the saving grace of God. He had been young, but he remembered her teaching him from the Bible. He had not always done the right things, but the knowledge and commitment were still with him. She had shaped his life without her even knowing it. Now he was having second thoughts about his reaction to her calls.

Her mention of his brothers in the letter had really caught him off guard. As each hour passed, the desire to see them grew stronger and stronger. He couldn't throw his kids a curveball now and tell them he'd been dishonest, but maybe one day they could handle it and understand. They would always have their grandparents, but he wasn't sure how his parents would take the idea of his wanting to rediscover his former life. Would they think him disloyal? He already knew how his wife would feel about it. She would strongly support any decision he made. He was going to think on this for a while, but he was reconsidering his options.

Maybe he would just send a simple message to his birth mother. No facts, no commitments, just enough to let her know he did indeed remember. He wanted to send a message that said, "Our family chain is broken, and nothing seems to be the same; but as God calls us one by one, the chain will be linked again." Yes, one day soon he would send that message.

After Frances' funeral, the boys went to her house to mingle with the guests and take one last time look at her home of these last dozen years. She didn't have much, just simple things that she treasured in her life, such as her mother's knitted afghans and her father's Bible. The only pictures were those taken the last ten or twelve years of William, Ted, Eddie and the families, and one of Art in uniform given to her by the Newman's. William picked up his mother's Bible sitting on the table by her chair to see where she had last been reading. He noted that in the front of the Bible, in faded ink, was the name of William McGrew and the date, July 1, 1895. He recognized it as the Bible his grandfather had given her when she graduated from the eighth grade and then had taken it back in anger. She had told him the story about that.

As he leafed through the worn pages, he came upon a bookmark and noted that it was placed in the 23rd. Psalm. "The Lord is my Shepherd...," and thought indeed he was for her. He was about to close the Bible when he noticed writing on the bookmarker. It read Leo Swenson – Rockford Illinois – 555-4242. He stuck it back into the Bible and told his brothers, "If you don't mind, I'll take this."

In life Frances had reunited these three sons, and they knew from that day on that they could always count on one another. They were as close as a phone call away. These last years they had truly learned the character and commitment of this woman who had given them birth. They owed her much for the sacrifices she made and the values she instilled in them at an early age.

After the funeral William went back to his home in Virginia, but had a sense of incompleteness that stayed with him for several months.

The circle had not been closed effectively. One day, using the phone number from his mother's Bible, he secured a Rockford address for Leo Swenson and sat down to write him a letter. It turned out to be a very long letter spelling out the courage of their birth mother, and the faith that this woman had, and the loyalty she had to each of her sons. He gave a detailed account of the reason for the adoptions and the betrayals she had faced in life with their father and others, while never losing her faith in God. He also went on to give an accounting of each of the boys and their lives, including his own. He closed with the comment, "Leo, I don't know what you do know or don't know about these past thirty years, but I remember the brother I shared my life with for ten years. Your mother prayed for you each day of your life, and prayed that one day she'd meet you again in heaven. Her last conscious thoughts were of her sons. Your brothers and I would love to see you and close the circle, but we will respect your wishes and privacy and never think any the less of you." It was signed, your brother, William. The letterhead on his stationery had all the addresses and phone numbers that Leo would need if he chose to respond.

Six weeks later, at the headstone of Arthur Newman in Terre Haute, Indiana, four brothers gathered. Leo Swenson, William Watson, Theodore Wainright, and Eddie Trapp.

The oldest, Leo, spoke first. "Let's join hands here over our fallen brother and honor him. Let's also honor our mother who never gave up on us.

Although our lives have taken different turns, the values our birth mother instilled in us has turned a tragedy into a victory this day. The circle that she so wanted to close, is now closed.

Our parents and loved ones are not dishonored by this tribute to our birth mother, but rather we also acknowledge what they did for us. Their contributions were added to the foundation that she gave us.

What we have accomplished in our lives, and that includes the life of this hero who lies here, is because she first loved us. I pray she is looking down with Art today, and nodding, and waiting to greet each of us in turn as God calls us home. God has blessed our mother and God has blessed us."

William was the last to speak that day at the gravesite, and he concluded with these words. "If we never meet again this side of heaven, we will meet on that beautiful shore."

THE END

Printed in the United States
59203LVS00005B/256-348